ATTACK ON THE RASHTRAPATI BHAWAN

ATTACK ON THE RASHTRAPATI BHAWAN

They were patriots,
now ready to attack India.

ANISH BEHL

Srishti
Publishers & Distributors

Srishti Publishers & Distributors
A unit of AJR Publishing LLP
212A, Peacock Lane
Shahpur Jat, New Delhi – 110 049

editorial@srishtipublishers.com

First published by
Srishti Publishers & Distributors in 2024

10 9 8 7 6 5 4 3 2 1

This book is dedicated to Sri Aurobindo Ghosh, India's leading light in our freedom struggle. May many more Indians become aware of his brilliance and his contribution to a spiritual India.

Also to my father Shri Raj Pal Behl, who toiled all his life fighting the system and when the Judicial system declared him a winner, he hardly had time to enjoy his moment in glory.

To Shri M.P. Panditji, our light in Pondicherry. He would urge me to write for many years. It took me a long time to realise how much I would enjoy writing.

To my mother Promila Behl, my much better half Chavi and our two – Ishani and Arvind. You give me the peace to move forward. Thank you!

the carpet at the earliest in order to mitigate damage to his career also had a big part to play in it.

Disowned by Somesh, Mahesh was powerless and I knew it was impossible for him to walk out free this time, without at least eight to ten years of prison-time, and that was enough for me. He looked baffled when I caught a glimpse of him on a news channel, probably to an extent that he had started having self-doubts over his innocence. He had absolutely no idea I had ghost-fucked him.

I did have a word with Shalini's parents and they were distraught. I was sorry for their loss, but I couldn't do much about it. They planned to move to the US along with Sia to be with Tanisha, which meant I wouldn't have to worry about Sia.

I wouldn't say I was very happy, but content, yes. There was an insane sense of gratification and serenity that prevailed my mind, my heart and every cell of my body. I was sure Myra was smiling from up among the stars and that, for me, mattered the most. Not to mention, fulfilling the promise I had made to Rey and myself to punish the guilty made me feel proud of myself.

What happened could have been averted, but who knew life would come to what it did. There couldn't be a more unfortunate man walking the planet than me. First, the universe took away Myra and then, Shalini. What made things worse for me was that I had to squeeze the life out of my first love to feed the universe's plan of delivering justice to my second one. If given a chance to go back in time, would I do things differently in case of Shalini? I don't think so. Myra was always the priority and for her soul to rest in peace, the *Law of Revenge* had to be upheld and the guilty had to be brought to book. The law comes first and everything else, later.

There were regrets that had immortalized themselves and I had to live with them, whether or not I blamed myself for my misfortune. But don't we all know that love and life are messy and take turns that none can foresee or understand, leaving behind a long trail of regrets in its wake. The best one can do is minimize the regrets and unflinchingly accept destiny. I had done just that and it was now time for a new beginning.

CHAPTER 1
THE RELUCTANT ARCHITECT

India
1900s

At the Coronation Durbar in 1911, the British monarch announced the movement of the seat of power from Calcutta to Delhi. A town planning committee appointed Edwin Lutyens as the chief architect to design a brand new Viceroy's residence. However, unknown to Lutyens, there was some power play in the home office. Some felt that he was too straight-jacketed and all his designs of country homes in the UK were similar. After some thought, Herbert Baker was appointed as well. Herbert, a few years senior to Edwin had enormous experience in several continents, including Africa. The work was divided – Lutyens was to design the Viceroy House, and Baker the twin secretariat buildings. No one could foresee the bitter battle of intellectual capital that would soon break out between the two.

****

Calcutta
1912

Prodipto Sengupta stared at the draft again. He had spent the last two weeks putting final touches to the designs of the Viceroy House. One of the three assistants selected by Edwin sahib and Herbert sahib after a short interview last year, Prodipto was just coming to terms with the working style of his two superiors. Both were geniuses in their own right, though he found Edwin a little whimsical and Herbert a little too balanced, perhaps even bordering on boring. After passing out of the prestigious AA School of Architecture, London in 1907, Prodipto had joined a local firm in London as junior draftsman. He soon discovered that his brown skin automatically moved him as the unofficial lunch warmer and paper cutter. He knew that moving back to India was inevitable and this was an amazing opportunity. In November 1911, he was appointed as assistant draftsman to the design team of the Delhi Project. He was elated that he would be working with names like Edwin and Herbert.

However, as they say, all good things must come to an end. Prodipto joined the Calcutta office in February 1912 and he soon knew he had entered a war zone. Edwin and Herbert just could not appreciate each other's design philosophy. Prodipto knew he was now stuck in the middle of this toxic relationship. They were only scheduled to come to India for a month each, only once a year. And their next visit was due in September.

His ninth draft had come back after Edwin marked some changes. The draft was almost murdered with red and green ink marks all across. Red meant 'You're a bloody idiot! Change the whole design!' and green meant 'Will be acceptable only if you change whatever was marked by green ink.' At a rough count Prodipto counted 92 red markings and 13 green. Prodipto realised it was already 6 p.m. He didn't have the courage or energy to start work on the next draft, so he rolled up the draft, and he exited the office in Chowringhee.

It was Thursday and he headed straight for the Ekla Café at the end of the road. The café was owned by his dear and childhood friend Prabal Bose. Prabal and he shared a passion for wrestling and had been a force to reckon with in school. The PP combo was a deadly school team and won almost all the *Akhara pratiyogitas* in Calcutta. Whilst Prodipto, the son of a rich trader, managed to pursue his academic interests, Prabal started helping with his father's café and went on to take over running it full time in 1909. After Prodipto returned to Calcutta, they had agreed to meet at least twice a week, on Thursdays and Sundays. Prodipto looked forward to these meetings which were a welcome break from his on-going stress of managing two pompous British bosses. Prabal had kept his wrestling interests alive and even sponsored a few kids in some large akharas. It wasn't surprising that the café was usually frequented by some very fit young men and discussions centred around diet and exercises. In addition, of course, who could stop the never-ending discussion around politics. Increasingly, Prodipto sensed the frustration of the young men in Ekla Café. The Anushilan Samiti, set up in 1902 was getting quite popular. While Prodipto did agree to the need for independence, he could not quite agree to the rising sense in the samiti that violence was the only way to the path of freedom.

We don't stand a chance, he thought. The ruthless actions of the British armed forces after the 1857 revolt could not be forgotten. How could he forget tales of bodies hanging from trees outside several villages. Contrary to general perception, the massacre perpetrated by the British army in 1857 to 1858 was hardly recorded in history. Sepoys accused of desertion were executed, their family members in villages were hunted down and men, women and children were hanged from trees in the villages. These tales of the carnage were also contributing to increasing chorus of violence. If anything, Prodipto guessed that Delhi, Punjab and Calcutta were at the forefront of these views.

The Anushilan Samiti was one such aggregation of young men, mostly from akharas around Calcutta. By 1902, Calcutta had three secret societies which openly supported the use of violence to get rid of the British in India. One was founded by Calcutta-based student Satish Chandra Basu with the patronage of Calcutta barrister Pramatha Mitra, while another was led by Sarala Devi, and the third founded by Harobindo Ghose. Ghose and his brother Barin were among the strongest proponents of militant Indian nationalism at the time. Nationalist writings and publications by Harobindo and Barin, including *Bande Mataram* and *Jugantar,* had a widespread influence on Bengal youth and helped Anushilan Samiti to gain popularity in Bengal. The 1905 Partition of Bengal stimulated radical nationalist sentiments in Bengal's *bhadralok* community, helping the samiti to acquire the support of the educated, politically-conscious members. The samiti's programme emphasised physical training that included training its recruits with daggers and lathis (bamboo staffs used as weapons).

Just as he reached the café, Prodipto noticed one of the key success factors of the popularity of Ekla Café sitting at the reception. Pavitra Bose, Prabal's younger and only sister was busy taking orders and recording them in the register. All of seventeen, Pavitra was a natural entrepreneur. Her business-like approach coupled with her rather risqué dress sense was quite the draw for the young lads.

"Namaskar, Dada," she remarked as soon she saw Prodipto entering.

Prodipto nodded, rushing straight in, trying his best not to glance at her. He knew it was a risk. She would usually give a coquettish smile and sometimes even a wink and that would be enough to make Prodipto so unsettled that he could hardly make any conversation after that.

"Dada... Dada..." She chased after him.

"Stop stop! Your friend isn't in today. Prabal da is at the crockery unit. He asked you to join him there. You know where it is, right?"

With Pavitra right in front of him, he could not but help look at her.

"Mmmm... sorry. Of course, the crockery unit. Oh okay... mmm... yes," he mumbled and tried slipping past her at the entrance.

"Calm down, Dada..."

She held his arm and he felt his blood rushing.

"You know how to get there, right? Just use the rear entrance."

Prodipto managed to rush out of the café. It took a minute's walk to calm him down.

Crockery shop? On their agreed date day? Prodipto cursed. He was going to miss his caramel custard. Damnit!

Five minutes later, he was at the rear entrance of the crockery unit. Prabal used the old warehouse to stock grains, cooking utensils and a few crockery sets. Prabal rotated all crockery sets every three months. It was an extra expense, but he felt it gave a feeling of novelty to the patrons. He went up the stairs and pushed the door, but it was locked.

"Hellooo Prabal? Open the damn door! Why the hell are you here today anyway?" he hollered. Gone was his British accent and the put on *pucca sahib* act. With Prabal he was always his natural self and that's what he loved as well.

"Open the door, Gorilla face!"

Suddenly, the door opened with speed, and before he could say anything, two arms grabbed him and pulled him inside. The act was so swift that Prodipto felt a crushing pain in his arms.

"What the... let go of me!"

"Shut up! Will you just shut up? Can't you just knock on the bloody door and wait?" The voice did not belong to Prabal.

"Whaaat... who are you?" Prodipto stared at the bearded youth in surprise.

"Relax... Dada... relax," he heard Prabal's voice from the end of the hall. It was dark and as his eyes got accustomed, he noticed three more men standing around a table.

"Meet my friends, Prodipto. I called you here as we didn't want to be seen in public. Say hello to Alankar, Amrit, Subhash and Alok."

Prodipto straightened up rubbing his biceps, glaring at the bearded guy called Alok. He noticed the other three were standing ramrod straight. Yes, definitely Akhara members. You can make out a well-toned body. Prodipto, still rubbing his arms, walked slowly to the group. Everyone nodded and shook hands.

"Gentlemen, meet my English sahib friend from London. This young man is a famous architect and chose to come back to dirty Calcutta. He is also a fellow wrestler and loved dangal as much as we all do. Of course, he has turned soft now..." Prabal poked Prodipto's ribs as he spoke.

"But I vouch for him and we can trust him."

The bearded one spoke,"Prabal, I hope so. You know I don't trust these government types. We will have to keep a watch on Mr Prodipto."

"Hold on... hold on. Trust? What is happening here? Prabal, I don't like this guy's attitude in any case. I don't know what you folks are cooking, but I don't want any part in it. See you ..." Prodipto turned around walking towards the door still nursing his arms.

"Wait... wait..." Prabal rushed to hold him by the arm.

"Just hear us out first, okay. Then you can walk away if you like," Prabal gently turned him around and moved to the main table.

On the table were three wooden boxes. They were well packaged, indicating they had been recently shipped or were being prepared for shipping.

Prabal nodded to the tall hulk in the green kurta. "Amrit, go ahead. Let's get to work, gentlemen."

Amrit was at least 6 feet 3 inches tall, quite a strange sight in Bengal where the average height was 5 feet 6 inches. Taking a long rod from the table, Amrit took one of the boxes and went to work, splitting the wooden structure that supported the box inside. In a matter of minutes, Amrit had torn apart the wooden beams and was now using a small axe to break open the core box. From the core box emerged a metallic case almost the size of a small travel case.

Amrit took the case out and handed to Prabal. "I think you have the keys, Prabal da," Amrit whispered. There was a strange silence in the room. Prodipto was transfixed and stared at the rather rich looking case. What is this now, he wondered.

Prabal took the case and fished out a box from his pocket, from which he took out a small key. He inserted the key into the main lock in the centre and with a loud spring action, the lock sprung open. With great flourish Prabal smiled and slowly, almost like he was carrying an expensive crystal vase, placed the case at the centre of the table.

"Amrit, you open it. You deserve it. You've worked hard. It's a privilege you deserve."

Amrit moved forward and opened the two side clips and threw the case open for everyone to see.

The tiny light bulb on top of the table was the one source of light and it shone on the contents in the case.

A collective gasp went around the room as the six men stared into the case. The case had a thick sheet of packing ribbons and placed in six slots were six steel containers with glass on the top so you could see clearly what was inside. In each box was a shiny small handgun. On top of the box was a folded piece of paper.

There was deathly silence in the room.

Handguns in India, and that too in 1912, were a rare sight. The British army did carry them, but they had the very old models with hammers. These were clearly the new hammerless models. Prodipto, coming from a wealthy family, was familiar with guns. His father had armed security, given that they had been attacked by sword-yielding thugs. But even he had never seen something this modern.

Moving slowly, almost with the love and tenderness of a newlywed groom, Amrit picked the paper on top of the case, opened it and read it aloud.

"The Colt Model 1903 Pocket Hammerless .32 ACP calibre, self-loading, semi-automatic pistol. Designed by John Browning and built by Colt-Patent Firearms Manufacturing Company of Hartford, Connecticut, USA. Six pieces ordered by M/s Indounion Traders, London."

Slowly, Prabal moved forward and opened one box and took the weapon out of its box. Holding it in his hand, he incredulously looked at Amrit and whispered, "*Tumi chamatkara... Amrit. Chamatkara*! You are a genius." He moved forward, pulling Amrit into a tight embrace. Prodipto saw all five move into a kind of a group hug. In unison, they shouted, "*Bande Mataram... Bande Mataram... Bande Mataram.*"

Amrit whispered, "Not me, Prabal da, not me. She is a genius. Misha is a genius."

Misha Alfa was a French revolutionary with Turkish heritage and had been a key supporter of the Indian freedom movement. Using various routes, she had been a key supplier of arms to the Indian underground movement. There were murmurs that she was even planning to set up a training centre in Pondicherry, a French colony in south of India.

Colt 1903. Wow! The export of this American handgun was banned till 1910. These had to be some of the first few pieces coming out. And to Calcutta... to Prabal. Just the thought was shocking for Prodipto.

The moment the group had chanted 'Bande Mataram', Prodipto's fears turned to cold admission that he was now in the company of freedom fighters. Prodipto felt for his nation equally; he felt the anger, the helplessness at being a second-grade citizen in his own country, but then the sheer routine of daily work numbed his thoughts and forced him to ignore the stark reality that faced him. His father had refused to provide food grains for the British army in 1901. The result was a complete ban on his activities by a trumped-up charge of sedition. The business went down and his father immediately made plans for Prodipto to move to London. Finally, his father's estate was auctioned by creditors and he died a pauper in 1908.

"Prabal, have you gone absolutely crazy? Guns in your crockery centre! Hammerless models... they must have cost a fortune. I don't want any part of this, Prabal, I told you. I am off!"

"It's time you realised who you are, Prodipto," Prabal whispered. "Was it not a wake-up call when the government killed your father? When he died of shock seeing the ancestral home being sold? Dying all alone when you were in London. Does it have no meaning for you?"

Prabal raised his voice. "Look around you, my friend, this is a cage. Your own home is a cage. We will not live in a cage; we will not live in peace while the whites take away our wealth!" Prabal almost shouted.

"Prabal, why are you showing me all of this now? You've been planning this for months, right? I moved a year back. *Why me? Why now?*" Prodipto cried agitatedly.

He was embroiled in this and he could see his life crumbling. He had Prabal's collar in his hand and he was sure he wanted to beat his face to pulp.

"Do you realise I am a government servant?" Prodipto whispered. He looked around and he saw terrorists. Good lord, would he have to report this? Anger welled up in him, and it focused on Prabal as he had involved him in a dangerous game.

"You swine! How dare you involve me in this stupid idea of yours. You think a few dozen guns will scare the empire away? You idiot!" Prodipto was inches away from Prabal.

"You coward. Here, take this, and use it!"

He handed the Colt to Prodipto and then put the gun to his temple.

Prodipto pressed the Colt against Prabal's forehead and in one action slid the action strip back, staring at Prabal with tears flowing down his cheeks

"Why me, Prabal? Why now? Tell me. You have destroyed my life. At least you should have discussed it with me. I am now a witness. Do you see that?" he whispered to his dearest friend. His hand with the gun slid down and he looked at the floor in sobs, breaking down.

Prabal put his arms around him and spoke softly.

"Because Prodipto, you are my brother and you are the guy designing the Viceroy House in Delhi."

Prodipto was shocked. So there was indeed some design in all of this. The Viceroy House ... how did Prabal know?

"How do you know this? I never mentioned it. How do you know?"

"Yes, you didn't tell me, my silly twat, but the girl you secretly love, Pavitra, asked you and you blabbered to her that you were designing the Viceroy House."

Prabal was silent, embarrassed that his feelings for Pavitra were so evident.

"I see... but what does this have to do with all of this?"

"You see, my dear member of the Anushilan Samiti, you will do what no other Indian can do. Give us access to the Viceroy House in Delhi."

Prodipto stammered, "Whaaat? How? I... Viceroy House access? I don't get it... I am not part of the security, you idiot. I only make drawings. Don't you understand? I am not some government officer who will give you a pass to enter the Viceroy House. And why do you even need access to the place?" Prodipto was shaking his fist in Prabal's face.

"You think the Viceroy will listen to your call for freedom, and sign a decree making us independent? Really, you friggin' dumb café owner! Wake up! What are you going to do? Smuggle a Colt in, and ask the Viceroy to free us?"

Prodipto was now staring at all the five men in the room with a look of sheer contempt.

"No, you are right, we don't want access to talk to the Viceroy." Prabal now stared at Prodipto with a serious deadpan look.

Amrit suddenly moved to Prodipto, putting both his hands on his shoulders, "We want access to the Viceroy House through a route that you will tell us. Mr Shaky Pants, a route that will get us inside the house..." and a pause ensued.

"To kill the Viceroy!"

CHAPTER 2
THE RELUCTANT REVOLUTIONARY

Calcutta
1912

The morning rays found Prodipto Sengupta awake in his bed at home. In a daze, he had walked back from Prabal's store the previous evening. He managed to shovel in a few spoons of food and claiming that he was having a headache, went straight to bed. His elder sister, his only sibling, was a widow, and after his return from London had moved in with him. He was grateful. He kept terrible hours and not once did she ever complain.

The previous evening's meeting with Prabal's friends had reminded him who he was and what was happening around him. Working with the British government sometimes made him forget the growing chorus for freedom in India. Born to a wealthy family, they never really had much trouble with the British. If anything, better law and order, rail connections and the like had only made the family wealthier. Of course, they never really were away from it all. The family's doctor had been Dr Ashhnadhan Ghosh. His father and the Doctor, called Krishna fondly by his father, had been friends for several years. The Doctor's entire requirements of food grains were organised by his family and this had bought the two families together.

The children too were of similar ages. Prodipto was friends with Krishna's four children, though he was closer to Biru and Harobindo. Prodipto had planned to take the Indian Civil Service exam, but decided on Architecture. Harobindo (Auro) was the smarter brother. Even as teenagers, Prodipto was inspired by Biru's fierce personality. Auro was the strong and silent types, while Biru was the firecracker. Later,the three of them were in UK as well together and had met up a a few times.

Prodipto could not help but think of the two as he was drawn to the movement on account of their influence on his entire thinking process. Sitting in Britain over cups of coffee, Biru would narrate his plans on how the British could be fought and pushed out of India.

"Prodipto, I ask you, have you ever fed food to a rabid dog?" Biru would ask such obvious questions that Prodipto could only but listen to him in awe. His plans were detailed and he would often look at Auro for acceptance. Auro would simply look at Biru and smile. He spoke rarely, but Prodipto felt drawn to him. Post his admission to AA School of Architecture in 1904, Prodipto lost touch. He would only hear from his family that both Auro and Biru were getting to be quite popular in the Anushilan Samiti back in India. They started some publications as well. One was called *'Jugantar'*. With circulation of over 20,000, the publication was even read in Dhaka. *Jugantar* contained written thoughts on armed revolution for Independence. Then, just before Prodipto came back, an earth-shattering event took place. Revolutionaries attempted to kill the Presidency Magistrate Douglas Kingsford in 1908. What followed in the investigation was that out of the several suspected individuals, twenty odd persons were caught at Biru's country house. Following this, Auro and Biru were also arrested. When this happened, Prodipto was grateful he had not responded to any of Biru's letters asking him to drop Architecture and join the Samiti. There was no way he was going to give up his career. The British empire had a huge footprint and there was terrific demand for architects. Anyway, he felt he couldn't really make a difference. After the 1857 revolt, the British had demonstrated they could be ruthless and unforgiving. He had ignored such calls to join these vagabonds and remained focused on his career.

He learnt that Auro had been sentenced for only a year and Biru for a longer term. Thank god he had stayed away from these chaps. Now that he was back, he could not ever imagine that he would once again come face to face with the revolution. Indeed, of all the people, his Prabal, the ever-sissy Prabal! Of course, he had noticed the makeover of feeble reed-thin Prabal after his return. He was certainly bulking up. He could see his thick arms and his tight jawline. Reading *Jugantar* was one thing, but organising arms, and that too a Colt 1903, was certainly out of bounds. Something more serious was brewing here and now he was, at least, an accessory to this knowledge. His mind raced and stomach churned.

He realised he was getting late. Pushing all his thoughts back, Prodipto rushed to work and in an hour was back at his design table unrolling the draft designs with the red and green markings made by his mentor.

The office had two other architects. A qualified professional with more than forty years of experience, Richard Walter was almost seventy years of age and was almost a relic. He had bad arthritis and found it difficult to move about. He would drop in only twice a week. The other person was David Alter. He was a trainee. He may have some link with Lutyens as he was specially sent for a year after completing only two years' studies. A break in the middle of a six-year study programme wasn't seen as a good mark on anyone's certificate. It indicated he had probably failed his second year, though David himself claimed he was quite an adventurer. They had one more staff member – Bullu, the office boy.

"Good morning, Pro," David muttered as he entered the office almost an hour late. A nervous wreck himself, for Prodipto, David was somebody he would love to slap around a bit and maybe break a leg sometime. Just twenty-three years old, the young twit had the audacity to address him as Pro. He had corrected him several times and that day was just the last straw that broke the camel's back.

"David!" Prodipto hollered."Could you step up here, please?"

David stopped mid step, turned around and went straight to Prodipto.

"Yes?"

"David, what time is it? Or have you misplaced your father's Roamer Swiss made watch?" Sarcasm dripped from his voice. David often took his pocket watch out with a flourish and had announced on numerous occasions that it was a Roamer.

David stared at Prodipto and looked just shocked at being spoken to like that.

"Look here, Pro. Just because I am a gentleman and all, that doesn't mean you can speak to me in that tone Mr Purodipto. Be very sure that I am here at Mr Lutyens' request and do *not* report to you. You should feel lucky I haven't reported your rather tardy work, if I may say so, to both Lutyens and Herbert. I report to Richard, who is our Chief Architect and you better be sure about that. So, stop checking on my timings that are none of your business and start getting some work done around here. While you are at this, please stop making those slurpy sounds while drinking that awful tea you keep ordering from the shop across. This isn't Park Street you know, this is an office of the British Architecture department. So please get your act together, else I may just get your brown posterior kicked out of this office!" saying this, David stared hard at Prodipto and stormed off to the next room.

In shock, Prodipto turned around to his table to hide the tears streaming down his cheeks. He stared at the draft design roll. He suddenly felt transported back to London, the only brown face in an office of ten British architects. The colour would never leave him, would it?

In the next room, he could hear laughter. Clearly, young David and Richard were enjoying themselves. While more Indians were absorbed in professional jobs in the empire, it was clear that they would always remain second class citizens. At this moment, all Prodipto was thinking was of going back to Prabal, borrowing one of the colts and taking care of Mr David. He imagined pointing the colt at him and pumping all eight bullets into his head. He had had enough of his insolent tone. If someone had asked him at that moment, he would be only too happy to kill the Viceroy himself, damn it!

By three in the afternoon, Prodipto had calmed himself and knew that his moment of anger had already washed away to his ever practical 'don't want any trouble' personality style. He was having a terrible headache. He grabbed his bag and the draft roll, thinking he'd finish it at night at home. He went in to the adjoining room to report to Richard.

"Sir, I am leaving. Bad headache. I will give you my corrections tomorrow morning."

Richard looked at him with pity. Slowly, he kept his drafting pencil down leaned back on his chair and stared at Prodipto.

"Sir, do allow me to leave. Not feeling well, I think," Prodipto said looking at the floor.

"Prodipto Sengupta, what rank were you in the AA School, my lad?"

"Huh... rank?" Prodipto was taken aback at this

"Yes, yes young man, what rank were you? Forgotten already, eh? Well, I haven't. I saw your profile and advised Lutyens you could be an asset to the team. Third in a class of thirty-five. Thirty-five of the best draftsmen in Europe and UK. Your work on the Thames bridge, of using motifs on the claddings was just brilliant. Lutyens personally told me he had not seen such innovation in a long time. I saw your work on the Delhi VH (Viceroy House). You are already getting acceptance on design, never mind the markings."

Prodipto was taken aback. Richard was a rather taciturn boss. Where was this going?

"Mr Sengupta, I love India. I love the food, the people and the variety. The biggest problem with you folks, my lad, is that you are serving yourself in a platter to the empire, aren't you? You are now conditioned to be the colonised race, the vanquished Indian. And you, dear sir, are just the perfect representation of the Indian people." Richard's voice was rising in tempo and decibels. His nostrils were flaring; his skin was getting pink.

"Mr Richard... I... er. I don't know what you mean. Have I done something wrong?"

"Have I done something wrong?" Richard mimicked in a shrill voice. He stumbled up from his chair leaning over towards Prodipto.

"You have bloody done something wrong, you bloody twat! If my son was ever shouted down by a young friggin' second year failure faggot and he kept quiet, I would take my knuckles to his face and give him a hiding, I would. You bloody sissy! How could you stand listening to that useless piece of shit? You are his senior, by Lord! Third bloody ranker from AA School. That's the problem with you Indians. All friggin' talk, no action. Keep doing 'namaskar' and keep your hands in your bloody pockets. So now you have a bloody headache, eh? Get the hell out of my face, you ass-licking bloody moron. Get a life and remember, Prodipto Sengupta..." Richard went silent and he raised his index finger right under Prodipto's nose,

"You want some respect, son, start respecting...." he paused, "... Yourself... you hear me? Start respecting yourself!"

He crumpled back into his chair.

"Now get out. *Get out!*"

A shaken Prodipto turned right about and almost ran out of the office.

He went straight home to his room and crashed on his four-pillared bed. It was his father's bed that he had managed to save in the auction. He had a life-sized portrait of his father just behind his bed.

What was happening? Why was this happening? Should I go back to London? Yes, I need to get out. Should I resign and move to Africa? He took his head in his hands and broke down completely. His body shook with his helpless crying. Richards' words were cutting into him far more than David's. He was used to that. That was normal. But Richard was the first Britisher who had spoken to him like this. How dare he. No respect? I'll teach him respect. Before he knew it, he had fallen into a deep slumber only to be woken up by knocking on the door a few hours later.

"Manko... Manko ... Are you asleep, Manko?"

Di was on the door knocking. Prodipto gulped some water down, got up and went to the door.

"Yes, *jiji*?"

"Uff... Baba. *Tumi ghumāccha kēna*?"

"No, Didi. Was having a headache."

"Why didn't you tell me, Manko?" She raised her palm to touch his forehead.

"Good, no fever. Come down, your friend is here. I have made coffee."

"Who, Di?" He hoped it wasn't Prabal. He'd throw him out.

"Is it Prabal, Di? Tell him I'm not well."

"Arre Baba, if it had been Prabal, he would have come up and broken down the door. Some nice-looking girl is here. She quite shyly said to tell you that what you ordered from Ekla Café is here. Did you order my favourite lemon tart now? Did you? I just love the tarts."

Prodipto was taken aback. Ekla Café? What did I order? Prabal must have sent the baker with some goodies to appease him.

"Di, just take the package and tell her to go. I really am not well." He must have spoken a little loudly as his voice carried over to the main living room.

"Prodiptoji, Prabal da asked me to deliver this. Can I please speak with you? Please I won't take long."

It was Pavitra. In his own house, Mr Architect suddenly went all nervous.

"Di, tell her I am coming down," he mumbled.

His sister smiled, "Aha, no headache now, eh?"

She giggled and went down to the porch.

Prodipto ran back to change his kurta. He splashed his favourite aftershave, ran the comb through his hair and rushed down.

As he walked down the staircase, he could see her petite frame on the large corner sofa. She was wearing a pastel green saree, her hair tightly knotted. He understood the English saying – 'a sight for sore eyes'.

He smiled as he approached her. Pavitra stood up and bowed slightly with a namaskar.

"Oh! Hello Pavitra. Nice to see you here."

"Prabal da was busy, but he wanted you to have this and this note in this envelope. He said you must open it when you are alone."

"Will you have some coffee?"

"I already had a cup. Jiji was so nice. I will leave now."

She stood up and as she went towards the door, she crossed Prodipto. As she passed him, her hands brushed his. Suddenly he could feel her fingers squeeze his wrist. She looked straight into his eyes and whispered, "Do come to Ekla Café tomorrow. I will wait for you."

Prodipto stared after her for some time even after she had left.

"Manko baba, she's gone. Wake up!"

"Oh no, no Di. I was just thinking," Prodipto took the package and the note up to his room as Didi smiled at him.

He reached his room and opened the envelope. It was clearly Prabal's handwriting.

If you insult my friend, you insult me.

Prodipto was puzzled, what was this? Some kind of trick by Prabal? Prodipto was sure Prabal had sent his favourite Balushi with jaggery as a token of apology. No wonder the idiot was scared to come himself. He smiled to himself. He was feeling better already. There was a note and a plastic see-through circular box. It had some cotton inside. He opened another note inside it.

David Alter met with a small accident at the coffee shop. He may not come to office for a few days. Do send him some flowers.

Prodipto was in shock. David Alter? How did Prabal know David? He opened the bangle box. He peered inside, but screamed and retreated. He jumped from his bed. With that, the box flew from his hands. And from the box, what was very clearly a bloody tooth, flew out and fell onto the floor. Prodipto was trembling. Was this the beginning of his life's worst nightmare?

CHAPTER 3
TAKING SHAPE

Calcutta
1912

Walking in a daze, Prodipto found his way to the café. He had taken a quick shower. His pulse was still racing. He saw Prabal at the counter. It was almost six in the evening and the crowds were dwindling. In any case, with the police on alert, any group of young men was marked and almost all participants had a tail assigned to them for weeks. Countrymen were spying on each other. Attractive rewards had turned many patriots into secret 'khabris'.

Standing outside the café, Prodipto caught Prabal's eye and they stared at each other for a few seconds. The aroma of fresh coffee was in the air but Prodipto could not smell the bread. Nahoum bakers had just lost a few young kitchen workers and Prabal had hired them recently. The Jew from Baghdad sure had some of the best breads and cakes in town, and now, Ekla café had a few of those items. One of them was the vanilla muffin. The hot muffin and strong chai was comfort food for Prodipto. Just the visual of the muffin and the chai overpowered Prodipto. He broke eye contact, walked into the café and ran up the stairs to find his favourite corner table. Before he even sat down, he heard Prabal shout to the kitchen, "Four vanilla muffins and two chais for table eight!"

In minutes, Prodipto saw Prabal carry the tray and walk across to the table. He sat down. Prodipto started to say something, but Prabal just held his hand and signalled him to stay quiet.

"Let's enjoy our chai, Manko. We have time to discuss life."

With that, the next fifteen minutes passed in complete silence. Each bite of the raisin-filled muffin sent waves of comfort down Prodipto's spine. The extra hot tea infused with cardamom calmed his panic-stricken mind. He could die for these muffins. As they drank their tea, Prodipto now noticed that he and Prabal were clutching each other's hands in a tight grip.

"Is he fine?" Prodipto asked.

Prabal looked up. He raised his eyebrows in a gesture of innocent query.

"Stop it, you son of a bitch! You know I am talking of the firangi, my colleague David."

Prodipto stared at him.

"He is fine; he was just taught a lesson. He 'accidentally' had a tiff with a few drunken lads. A few bruises and the loss of a fine tooth. Tsk tsk tsk... one should be careful of drunk groups of boisterous young men. You agree? You can't harass my closest friend in Calcutta and get away with it, can you, huh?"

"How did you know this? Who told you?" Prodipto was calm now.

"Dada, welcome to the new Bharat. We have eyes everywhere. I know you have been to England. It's over now, Manko. We want free air. Look what happened to your own father. Are you really at peace with it? Freedom comes at a price. We have been working for years now. By the way, how did you think Lutyens chose you to assist him. Barin Gosh and Harobindo have been helping with logistical support in England. Armed struggle is now our responsibility. The pistols you saw... you think they come cheap? We have rich patrons. Individuals and even governments. Barin had already figured out how to organise explosive making training groups in France who were willing to do the same in India. A Turkish bomb maker in Paris is our official trainer. Haro is now in Pondicherry. He does some spiritual work, but he is the most ardent supporter of armed struggle. In fact, one of the chief strategists from France, Misha, is also in Pondicherry helping us. Pondicherry is a French colony and a number of revolutionaries have found a haven there, away from the Indian police. While you don't know much, Prodipto, we are large in numbers. Bengal has led the way."

"Hmmm. You mean I am here because this so-called 'freedom group' wanted me here?"

"No, Manko. We just made sure they selected you for this project. Coming here was destiny. We thought Lutyens would keep you there. We did want that you stayed there, but it's good that he sent you here. We can now engage with you closely—"

"You mean use me."

"Use you? For what? You think I am making myself some fancy bungalow, Mr Cheeky Architect, that I can use you?"

Prabal's voice now quivered with anger. He had had enough of this attitude.

"Mr Prodipto, no one can force you. If you want to live your life, in denial to what is happening to your country; if you want to continue to have glasses of sherry with the lads who are raping your country, so be it. If you believe your father died of his own happy will, wake up. And if you are still happy living in peace in spite of this knowledge, so be it. I thought it wouldn't take much to convince you and you still had some Indian blood in your veins. I think I was wrong. Let's end this now. I am off. I have to run the café as well. Good night and get lost!"

Prabal got up from his table to walk away when suddenly Prodipto sprang up from his chair and landed a resounding slap on Prabal's face

"You bastard, you think I am happy knowing what the firangis did to my father..." he hissed and slapped Prabal repeatedly till he was hyperventilating.

Prabal suddenly grabbed Prodipto with both hands and enveloped him in a massive bear hug. Prodipto broke down in hysterical sobs onto his dear friend's shoulder.

Prabal held him tighter. A minute later, he whispered, "Go home, my brother. Go home and sleep. We will talk tomorrow in the same place where we unboxed the cakes. You get it. The cakes!" Prabal winked.

Prodipto used the tissues on the table to clean his face. He nodded and gave Prabal a tight hug and walked straight home.

***

After a quick shower, he told Di he had had a heavy snack at Ekla Café and would skip dinner. He was asleep as soon as he hit the bed. He fell into a deep slumber enveloped in peace that he had never felt before. He now knew what was missing in his life. Why he had felt as if he was living a life of artificial comfort. He now knew that he had finally joined the ranks of the Anushilan Samiti.

Next day, he wrote an application for a sick leave and sent it to his office. He wrote that he has severe diarrhoea and he would report to work once he felt better. He wore a large hat and walked to Ekla Café. After picking up Prabal, they walked to the warehouse.

Alankar and Amrit were already in the warehouse, bent over the large centre table that had several maps opened on it. There was no sign of the colts.

They all nodded to each other. Prabal spoke.

"Friends, today I am delighted that our team has now the expertise to create the most important weapon that we can ever dream of building. I wish Baru da and Haro da were here. This is bigger than any explosive we've made. The best French expert or Japanese support cannot make this weapon. It will be a weapon made by my brother Prodipto...."

Prodipto looked sheepishly towards the floor. Such praise always embarrassed him.

Prabal continued, "He has now drawn up the plans for this weapon, which will enable us to get into the Viceroy House, the pride of the British. We will assassinate the Viceroy in the Viceroy House in New Delhi, British India's new capital."

Prodipto looked sheepish. Truth be told, he did not have the faintest idea of what plans Prabal was talking about. He could see that he was spinning a story around Prodipto so that other team members extended some respect.

Who could have dreamt of this? Prodipto had to plan out an incredible feat, which if successful, would be the source for many a historian to write reams and reams about. The team looked at Prodipto in awe.

"Gentleman..." Prodipto addressed the team. He had to be honest.

"I have, last night, seen the current state of plans of the VH. There is no way that I can plant or design an access for two main reasons: one, the entire area is dug up for the VH and the ancillary building coming around it, and secondly, I have no experience in designing any such structure. While you may think that I must be a downright idiot not to know how to design some secret access, please be aware that what we are talking is not a normal access. It cannot be visible, so it has to be underground, which is also impossible. Almost all foundations now use a new material called 'cement' mixed with steel rods. This is an amazing combination and almost impossible to dig using normal tools. The VH is using the skills of Frenchman Francois Coignet, who added steel rods to prevent the exterior walls from spreading, and later used them as flexural elements. Luckily, I know Monsieur Coignet from my days in London and Prabal plans to use one of our contacts in France to have him advise us on the tunnel design. I have given this much thought and the one and *only* way for us to build this underground 'tunnel' is if Mr Lutyens requests for it. So all I have to do is make sure Lutyens designs the tunnel, gets the Frenchman to give advice on structure and execute it alongside the construction of the VH. All very simple, isn't it?"

The team looked at each other and were now rather sceptical of Prodipto's claims. He had no experience of this and looked rather immature, they thought.

Prodipto was looking at his new 'friends'. Did they miss the sarcasm? he thought to himself.

Prabal was the first one who spoke.

"Prodipto, you are quite a nitwit, aren't you? This is your so-called brilliant plan? Just asking Lutyens to do everything for you? Are you bloody mad?" Prabal was shouting now at Prodipto.

Frankly, Prodipto had no idea how he would do this. But why share the truth with his new-found friends, right?

"Prabal, trust me. I have everything worked out. This will be an action that will get us our freedom, my friend. We will call it the..." Prodipto mumbled to himself.

"Yes, we will call it the 'Swatantra Tunnel'... 'The Freedom Tunnel'."

As applause broke out. Only Prabal knew that Prodipto had been spinning a yarn. He slowly shook his head as Prodipto basked in glory. All he had to do now was the impossible.

CHAPTER 4
THE KINGS' ESCAPE

Calcutta
1912

After several meetings with the Anushilan Samiti members, Prodipto had requested that he be given six weeks to finalise the plan. To be honest, he had not been talking nonsense. He did have a plan, but he just wanted to be sure how it would be implemented.

For centuries, designers of the dwellings of the wealthy and nobles knew of an important part of any such unit. It was called the 'King's Escape'. This was a structure built along with the foundation and only a chosen few knew of the structure. A secret passage was built that the king and his close group – family, ministers and friends – would use to escape in case of a siege or an attack. The construction of such tunnels was an art in itself. There were a class of architects who specialised in such construction. The tunnels had to have ventilation without having visible openings, an ability to store food, ability to store sources of light and weapons. Some designs even had the ability for horses to be maintained at all times so the escaping king could use them for better speed.

As was common in architecture courses, a special part of the course, should the student opt for it, was the 'nobility protection designs'. Prodipto called it serendipity that he was offered this course as there was shortfall in students who opted for this programme. In three months, he learnt an amazing array of developments in this field. Research in cement had been incredible and the French were leading the way. Specially designed material that was water resistant as well as controlled the flow of sound were some of the incredible features of the course.

"This isn't simple, Dada!" Prodipto addressed the team, "It will need enormous resources. Labour, special cement, steel rods, and design approvals. How can it be done hidden from the British?"

"What do you want me to do? Write to Lutyens and ask him to design it for us?"

"Please give me time."

After four days of 'sick' leave, Prodipto returned to work early at nine a.m.

Bullu, the office boy, was cleaning his desk. Prodipto nodded at him and reached out to shake his hand. He had learnt that Bullu was a part of the samiti and Prabal had had him placed in the office to look out for Prodipto. Bullu was illiterate and his short stature somehow hid his muscle-bound toned athletic build. Bullu had informed Prabal of the altercation with Alter. Prodipto kept his bag on the rack, and after ten minutes, went in straight to Richard Walter's office.

"Good morning, sir!"

He noted Richard was busy dusting his small collection of miniature Kali paintings. Richard was fond of Indian artwork, especially paintings, and would often stay late, working on some of his watercolours. He was a keen donor to the Calcutta School of Art, where local artists were trained in

European art techniques. Richard had come across a unique art in Bengal which used the birds' feathers to depict various forms of Goddess Kali. He must have collected at least 10 such pieces. Every day he would lovingly take them out, clean them and keep them back on his mantlepiece. Prodipto was quite fond of Richard. He often thought that his love for Indian art, people and even food, almost made him an Indian with a British accent!

"Ah, Pro, my boy, good to have you back. We are drowned in work, you know. Lutyens and Baker have been fighting over the last few days. But, tell me, how are you?"

Before he could answer, Richard continued,

"You fell sick and then young Alter reported he fell off his bicycle and was laid up in bed, poor chap."

"Not so poor, actually after how he treated you, eh?" Richard giggled at Prodipto.

Prodipto felt the blood draining from his face, but kept calm and just looked back at him blankly.

"Oh, really? That is sad, sir. I know he did cross a line the other day, but he is an immature kid. I didn't pay too much attention. I hope he joins soon."

"A child he is, indeed," Richard responded. "The child has applied for a month's sick leave. Can you believe that? A fall from the bicycle and a month's leave. Disgusting attitude, if you ask me. If I had my way, I would take a stick to his behind, you know. Anyway, Pro, we have to catch up on work. Why don't you go through the messages L and B sent to us and then let's discuss them at say 12 noon over some tea and some scones. Aah, the ones Bullu gets from a café. Splendid then. Let's get on with it, mate."

Prodipto went back to his office and as soon as he opened the drafts sent back from London, he was at once drawn to a long, scribbled message by Howard Baker. Given that the two of them were working on the project, it was quite amusing to see how they took digs at each other through witty comments on the drafts. To ensure that a draftsman like him did not get confused, it was agreed that Lutyens would use a green coloured pencil and Baker would use a pink coloured one just so that everyone knew who was writing what. Every draft was going thorough painful iterations as the disagreements between the two architects would never end.

It was just amusing how such senior architects were behaving like children. Prodipto worked on the comments, marking up a new canvas that his team had made for him. His design strokes were masterful. By now, his hands could trace a perfect line or a curve with a given radius with amazing dexterity. You could use tools later to check, but Prodipto had a gift for this. It was often joked that one shouldn't bother using 'Ds'; if Master Draftsman Prodipto said the angle was 18 degrees, then it was 18 degrees.

At 12 sharp, Bullu came in and informed him that Richard Sahib was waiting for him in the pantry. After three hours of hard work, he was ready for a break.

Richard was already pouring tea and he looked up at Prodipto and smiled.

"Aha, my master craftsman. Come come. Look at what Bullu got us today. Have you tried this mava cake? And those scones are to die for..."

"Indeed sir, looks amazing."

He sat down and the next half an hour was an interesting discussion around how Richard had adopted four artists from a temple twenty miles away and was supporting them financially. In return he was getting them to paint ten Kali paintings.

Prodipto stared at Richard. What a wonderful person Richard was. And good at his work as well. The discussion veered towards Lutyens and Baker.

"Did you see the remarks? This project is doomed. Every single comment is being discussed over two-three months. How will it ever take shape? Frankly, I think soon they will give up and they should simply divide up work, so one doesn't know what the other is doing. This way is the the only way. In fact, you know this way, we can just about design a Kali mandir in the middle without any of Lutyens or Baker knowing about it." Richard laughed, winking at Prodipto.

Prodipto visualised a Kali temple in the middle of the viceroy house. He smiled at Richard's wit. A kali temple designed because of the conflict between the two host architects!

And then it suddenly dawned on him in a second. Richard had just solved his problem. He knew now how to put the tunnel in the plans. Richard, you're a genius! He thought to himself. It was simple. The Viceroy House needed a 'king's escape'. He knew this was god's way of showing him the path forward.

Richard spoke with childlike excitement.

"By the way, see what I have with me today. A brand new camera that doesn't need fuse lights to go off each time. Amazing technology. Come now, my boy, we must have a picture."

He had called out to Bullu and soon they were both posing at Richard's table. Bullu clicked the shutter. A few days later, Prodipto found a beautiful print of the picture in a wood frame at his house. It was now on the wall right in front of his study table.

CHAPTER 5
CIVILIZATIONS

New Delhi
2015

The picture was black and white, and was a 9 by 6 inch print. It was in an antique looking frame in a middle-class home in Delhi. It had a young Indian in glasses along with an elderly white man. Just below the photograph was a handwritten remark 'To my young Genius... from Richard'. The picture had certainly stood the test of time. It was lucky that it had been framed in a tight, glass-mounted frame that prevented oxidation. Just across the room was a forty-five-year-old man talking on his phone. Akram Khan worked with the Research and Analysis department, Government of India and was getting an update from his colleague.

"Yes Sammy, am on the way. See you, buddy.".

The caller, Samdup Jigme, was born in the Civil Lines hospital in Dharamsala in the northern state of Himachal Pradesh. Dharamsala, a hill station in India, was a popular tourist hotspot as the Dalai Lama, the spiritual leader of the Tibetans lived in a monastery in Mcleodganj, just above Dharamsala. Born in 1975, and now nearly forty years of age, Samdup ran the Centre for Tibetan Refugees at Lodhi Road. After the Tibetan refugee crisis in India, when large numbers of Tibetans escaped from Tibet to India, the state of Tibetans in India now was rather sad. They were treated as foreigners and India had to continue to balance Chinese and Tibetan interests. But the Tibetans always ended up on the shorter side of the bargain. The number of Tibetans in India has reduced drastically. Some say that in the last eight years or so, almost half of the Tibetan population had left India.

The frustration of the lack of Indian support coupled with the racial slurs cast by the local population led to a number of conflicts, specially in Dharamsala. Locals felt the Indian government continued to provide funds for a population that they felt was 'lazy', 'didn't take a bath' and 'ate dogs'. 'Bloody chinkis' they were often called. Tibetans felt let down by lack of employment opportunities.

Samdup's real role in India was, however, a little different. In 2000, the Research and Analysis Wing (RAW) a la CIA of India set up a special unit to look at building a network to infiltrate Chinese territory. Two young men, Akram Khan and Vishal Anand were tasked to execute the project. RAW figured that the Tibetans had closest resemblance to the southern Chinese diaspora. Most would still have some connection to Chinese residents. In addition, recruits were also from the north-eastern sectors of India. After having been in operational mode for almost fifteen years, the project had been revived in high flow mode since 2015. Deep infiltration of a territory has a long gestation lag if the operation has to have sound success rate. Infiltrating a population required integrating with the local population and then developing local assets. The effective 'boots on ground' were numbered at eighteen with an additional twenty-strong team as Admin and Central handlers, monitoring and putting information together. Of the eighteen, almost twelve task force members were drawn from the Tibetan diaspora. Samdup Jigme was a senior administrator of the project in Delhi with a day job of looking after the Tibetan centre as a cover. Project Chexo, named after a Tibetan dish, was now on high flow mode. This meant that the eighteen assets were well-entrenched in the Chinese population. In fact, out of the eighteen, three were even absorbed by the local political party and were part of brainstorming sessions. These were, in a manner, Indian sleeper cells in China.

Samdup and Akram were close friends now. Over the last several years, their families too had met and come close. Samdup's son Dorje practically lived at Akram Uncle's house. He studied at the University of Delhi and Akram wouldn't let him eat all his meals outside. Akram loved Dorje dearly. So, the Akram household had an adopted son who would drop in once in three days to eat home-cooked food. What's more, Akram's daughter Anjali was very close to Samdup's wife Perma, while Samdup's younger brother was one of the assets of Project Chexo.

From an early age, Dorje had taken a fascination to the insurance industry. To earn some money, he enrolled as an agent with Tata-AIA Life insurance company. The company had outstanding promoters in the form of Tatas and the AIA group. He attended a seminar by the company and it was a turning point in his life. It was natural for someone to find the whole discussion about death rather uncomfortable. The top 5 insurance companies' seminars were brilliant in sharing concepts around how this was to be done. The very basis of life insurance had impressed Dorje's young mind. Helping strangers protect their families was akin to social service for him. The emotional appeal of the product had him hooked and he was coming up as an impressive sales agent. WIth more than 40 insurance companies in India, he had realised that working with the largest in scale was immensely helpful. In life insurance, he had decided to only work with TATA AIA, ICICI Prudential and Bajaj Allianz. He analysed they had the best products in town for customers. They had strong promoters and would be around for many many decades and this would give comfort to any customer. He would often try to convince Anjali to enrol as an agent, but she found insurance sellers irritatingly persistent.

This project had given Akram a close look at the Tibetan tragedy in India. Mere pawns in the Indo-China politics, it was true that when elephants fight, the grass suffers. Getting to know Samdup and Tibetan culture had been a fantastic experience. Of all the operatives he had worked with, he found Tibetans extremely disciplined and loyal to the team. He could recall Sam Manekshaw's description of the brave Gorkhas and he saw several similarities. It was terrible, of course, how the Indian government treated them. He had sworn that he would do something for his team, and most certainly for Samdup.

Project Chexo had been allocated 10,000 sq feet space with full access to the RAW and NSA data rooms. NSA (National Security Agency) was the prime intelligence unit coordinating activities with all intelligence entities in India. The Project Chexo unit was housed in the same building as NSA, near Connaught Place in Delhi.

Walking into the office building, Akram was somewhat anxious. Leo had not checked in the previous day and that was odd. Leo had been placed in Beijing about nine years back, and he had never missed his weekly check in. Breezing through security and a quick ride up to the 15th floor, Akram ran straight to Samdup's office.

"Good morning, Sam... Any news?"

Samdup loved Akram like his own brother. Even though he was his boss, he loved Akram's sense of ownership to the field agents. He took responsibility of the eighteen agents on the ground.

"Hi Akram, relax. I just saw his check in message on the MRTS (Message Relay Transponder System) server. His laptop crashed so he had to wait to access a public unit. Was just about to call you. He is fine and he chose the symbol for 'Am fine and doing well' rather than just 'Am fine'.

This essentially meant that he was in play now and soon some information would flow through the MRTS. This was a satellite based encrypted communication protocol that was secure. Operating in China, the unit knew of the Chinese digital strength and had to be very careful when communicating with CP (Connaught Place) for information flow.

"Ah, thanks! That's great news."

"Sure, Boss. Was relieved as well. We have some great info today for review. Let's set it up for 3 p.m. and we can get MHA (Ministry of Home Affairs) and RAW Spoc (Single point of contact) to also attend."

"Aha, yes, have to invite those guys as well. Of course, they have bloody no value add, but just some more bureaucratic nonsense. Go ahead and do it."

The MHA defence centre allocated Spoc was Dr Aalok Singh (nicknamed Minspoc) and the RAW Spoc was Freddy Daruwala (nicknamed RAWSpoc). Spocs were critical positions and were the only ones authorised to engage with other departments, etc. Given the sensitivity of information, inter department Spocs were usually privileged appointments.

Akram went back to his office in a far more relaxed mood. He went over the e-handouts for the meeting. Information flow for these meetings was through specially designed Tabs. Controllers had full control of every Tab and once the information was glanced at, the documents were deleted. The Spocs had tabs as well. His phone alarm went off. Glancing down he exclaimed, "Oops! Puja at 5. Better be on time." Aarti, his wife had organised a Satyanarayan puja and the neighbours had been invited. Akram murmured to himself. If he missed it today, he would be in deep trouble.

At 3 p.m., the team was put together in the Central Review room. The review room had state of the art communication systems. It had several security features that prevented anyone from taking information out of the room. By regulations, all mobile phones were regulated by a home-grown app that mirrored every key stroke/ activity on a central server monitored by eight internal security officers. The room had a giant 65-inch screen in the middle and two side screens for guests to join through video links.

It was almost 3.06 and the two Spocs were yet to join. Samdup was looking at the e-handouts whispering instructions to Kyle. Samdup's right hand man was a ferocious Tibetan, Kyle. Kyle was a training specialist for hand-to-hand combat. He was a Master of Sengueï Ngaro, which meant 'the lion's roar', a traditional Tibetan martial art. This art specialised in using anything that was available at the site of battle. This martial art form was born in the Kham region of Tibet and secretly went down its ancestors' line of warrior monks from the 17th century until 1956, when Chinese soldiers destroyed the monastery that was the central training centre and massacred all the monks. Ten monks were saved a day before the attack and reached Dharamsala along with the Dalai Lama. Since then, the Mcleodganj monastery had a secret basement built like a bunker where Tibetan youth were trained in the martial art form. It was said that trained warriors could convert a handful of grass to be used like a blade. Kyle's core programme had been to ensure that all the Project Chexo implants were trained in this art form. He now spent most of his time in office, assisting Samdup.

Kyle turned to Samdup, "Should we just begin, boss?"

Akram reacted, "Yes, let's please do that. We can't keep waiting."

Just at that moment, the side screens flickered with activity and the video link established connection. Both the Spocs were in the same office.

"Hello there!"

"Hello sir. We are just about to start. Kyle, let's go," Akram looked at Kyle.

"Just a minute, Akram sahib." The Minspock raised his hand. "We had a meeting today and I am tasked to ask you these questions before we start. Is that okay?"

Akram was flustered. More budget questions, damnit!

"No issues, sir. Go ahead. We have all the time in the world," he sniggered with contempt.

"Mr Akram, in total, how many implants do we have now?"

Akram was taken aback.

"Hmmm, why would you want that information, sir?"

"Mr Akram, please respond."

"Eighteen. We had thirty-six, but some had to be extracted over the last five years."

"Okay, Mr Akram. How many TCRs (Target Country Residents) have these implants enrolled into the programme?" TCRs were local residents that the implants managed to enroll by cash or kind, or blackmail and sometimes even sex.

Akram was getting furious. All this was highly confidential data and he wasn't sure where this was going.

"Sir, as of now we have almost 228 TCR enrolments."

"And, Mr Akram, how many have infiltrated the defence establishment? Please share locations of these assets."

That was just enough for Akram

"I am sorry sir, but this is highly confidential information. We will share all the information that the Project collects, but the information of our assets and their recruits cannot be shared with you. I do hope you will understand."

Freddy Daruwala, the RAW Spoc came closer to the camera.

"Akram, you are part of RAW and anything that is asked for cannot be refused. Do you understand?"

"Mr Daruwala, Project Chexo uses foreign assets. And as per the project principles signed by our RAW Chief, this data is available only to three people in the world. As Project Director, yours truly, the RAW Director General and the

President of India. You, sir, will have to get an ordinance passed to get this information. You actually don't need this information, and should focus on the information rather than how it is being procured.

Freddy Daruwala had a lovely complexion. Even at fifty-eight years of age, he had rosy cheeks. Akram's remarks had an immediate impact on his complexion as he turned purple with rage.

"Mr Khan, you don't need to remind me about project guidelines. As Operations Head of the Far East sector, this project reports to me and you have no authority to refuse this or any information about this project. Mr Khan, you do know I have a very poor opinion of the information you have provided over the last few years. I don't want to go to the budget issues that we fought about last time. Please respond with accurate answers to these queries."

"Freddy, what the f*** are you talking about?"

Akram and Freddy were batchmates, though different in age. But then, six years back, riding on the success of a RAW operation, Freddy had gone up a few ranks and was now the boss on paper for Akram. Freddy had risen from the ranks whereas Akram being an IPS intake, had reached Freddy's grade at a fast pace.

Akram noticed the crimson colour Freddy's cheeks had taken at Akram using his first name.

He continued.

"Freddy, Freddy, Freddy... why are we doing this in front of this audience? We have some exciting information to share and let's look at that. If we want to discuss other matters, I can come over tomorrow."

RAW Spoc stood up and one could see his full six foot frame.

"Mr Akram, will you just answer the bloody questions right now?" The RAW Spoc was now screaming and it looked like he was having a cardiac episode of sorts. In full view of the members of Project Chexo, he was almost drooling with anger.

Akram stared at this team and then back at Mr Daruwala.

"Mr Daruwala, while you were behaving like a child in front of the entire team, I was just checking the project set up security protocol document."

The SPD for any project was a document signed in blood that gave clear access rights to various designations. Running operatives in other countries was no simple task. If this information leaked, agents could lose their lives, thereby reducing the chances of attracting more operatives. In view of this, the SPD was extremely protective of information regarding assets in foreign countries. Sometimes, even the head of RAW could not access this. Whilst the information sourced could be accessed across several units, the source of information was protected.

Akram was reading from his Security Tab.

"Mr Daruwala, as I read this document, I see that you are not allowed access even to this document. I regret that the information you ask for is protected under the SPD and I WILL NOT, please read my lips, Mr Daruwalla, WILL NOT, release the information you have asked for. What's more, the mere fact that you and the Minspock have sought this information from me allows me to raise an Amber Flag on this attempt to get this information that you or Minspock have no authority to access. I will escalate this to the escalation matrix for Amber flags for an independent investigation as to why you gentlemen are seeking this information. This meeting, sir, is over!"

With this, Akram moved towards the remote in front of him to disconnect the call.

"Akram, you bast—"

And Akram shut the video link down.

There was silence in the room.

That didn't go well, Akram thought. Freddy always managed to get his worst side out. But he was really worried. What was going on here? He looked at Kyle.

"K, go to the Nerd Techs, warn them of innocent request worm attempts on the mainframe. Be prepared."

Nerd Techs were about forty youngsters recruited by their technology head who himself was all of thirty-one years old. They included some of India's finest hackers as well as data security system specialists. Something was happening and Akram was alarmed.

"Sammy." Akram looked at Samdup. "Move to security stage 2."

The project had five stages of alarms. At stage 2, assets in foreign countries were sent a message to stay low for a week.

His phone buzzed and he saw 'Boss' flashing. That was Aarti. He showed the flashing phone to Samdup, who only smiled. When Samdup had met Akram's wife, he was surprised to find that she was a practising Hindu. He was, at first, surprised that Akram had a Hindu wife, but when he got to know Akram better, he realised what an interesting mixed ancestry he had.

Akram murmured, “Shit.... missed the puja again.”

Akram had met Aarti in college and they had agreed to never try and force their religion on each other. He had always worried that their children may have a tough time to decide which path to choose, but their only daughter had decided to be an atheist. He was fine with it. Religion, for him had only been a tool for peace and it didn’t matter who you prayed to. Sometimes Akram wasn’t sure even he was Muslim, Hindu or a mix. It was a happy problem, he smiled to himself.

CHAPTER 6
RESEARCH AND ANALYSIS WING CENTRAL OPERATIONS OFFICE

New Delhi
2015

Director General, R.K. Swamy stared at the small group of five that had come together in response to Freddy Daruwala's request. Swamy was a year away from retirement and all he wanted was to spend the next twelve months in peace. After forty years of service, he looked forward to going back to Jaipur and settling down peacefully. He saw Freddy's grumpy face and knew he was in deep stress. Freddy looked after the far-east ops and was the perfect RAW employee. Given the political wind, he could change any policy paper to turn either way. In India, it was ever so valuable to stick to the country's political agenda. Who the heck wanted to get transferred to Slovenia, pushing papers at a paltry salary?

The room had three more members, including their documentation chief who handled protocol, law and maneuvered the complex worlds of Indian jurisprudence. RAW had three types of operations – covert, stealth and dark. Stealth and dark modes were beyond Indian law and were not even recorded in formal data systems. RAW had a dynamic system of assessing its teams. Irrespective of rank, the established system allocated risk ratings to officers, depending on their psychometric profile. This was done annually. Unfortunately, Freddy, apart from being a lovely person, had a rather 'challenging' score on this count.

Even before everyone sat down, Freddy Daruwala wasted no time and took off.

"I want Akram Khan suspended from Project Chexo. He has attitude issues and is blocking requests for information from the Central Defence Coordinator in the PM's Office."

In a minute, Freddy had narrated his tale of woe, in quite a childlike way. Swamy stared at Freddy with a sense of disappointment. No wonder his psyche scores were poor. No self-control at all.

Swamy waited for Freddy to finish and then responded in an almost spiritual, calm tone.

"Freddy, before you asked for this meeting, the team went through the Tab recording of your meeting and let me ask Kaul (Mr Kaul was the documentation chief) for his view. What say, Kaul?"

Mr Yoginder Kaul was deputed from Army Intelligence five years back and had done an amazing job. Unknown to the public, the documentation head in RAW operations also saw the documentation of projects overseas. Creating legal entities in target countries was his forte.

"Swamy ji, I have already gone through the Tab recording. As you do know, Project Chexo is status 'Dark' project. Frankly, even I don't have rights to the details Freddyji is asking. As far as Mr Khan's stance is concerned, we can certainly put a mention in his Confidential Report of speaking rudely to his senior. However, as far as facts go, every single clarification Mr Khan has given is absolutely accurate. I have gone through the Project Mandate; Dark projects allow the Project Chief to have *absolute* command on the information flow from his project. If we can substantiate that the project is not providing information, we can shut down the project and all assets will be withdrawn, but there is no way that we can access information about assets. In fact, Swamy ji, Mr Akram Khans's escalation is also in keeping with Dark project policy. He has the right to refuse information to any individual he feels suspicious about."

Swamy absorbed this. It was a pity Freddy had let his personal feelings about Khan override his position in RAW. Freddy had indeed stepped over the line. He had no business asking for locations and the numbers of assets that Akram ran.

He looked at Freddy. "Freddy, my dear. You do know the Dark project policy, right? Am afraid this meeting's agenda is not to find ways to push Akram, but to request you to share with Mr Kaul, what were you doing breaking protocol and asking information about assets?"

Freddy stared around the room. He had called for the meeting and now he was being interrogated. He felt his face warm up, but he controlled himself and responded.

"The CDC (Chief Defence Controller) in PM's office asked me to furnish this information to the PM. He did not say why. He said it was confidential."

Director Swamy was taken aback at this information. Why did the CDC not alert him? Why ask Freddy information which he knew Freddy had no authority to get.

"Freddy, you did not log this request in the inter-department query system?" As information was always controlled and access right very detailed, RAW had a process to respond to any query by another government department or officer. All staff members were instructed to enter queries in a system, await the response from the Response Controller and then relay exactly the information that was supplied from the system. This left a strong trail of the demand and supply of information. The department was well aware of how systemic tracking of demands of information had also been helpful in identifying red flags and individuals who may be acting without authority. In the past, at least two spy rings had been busted by RAW using query analytics.

Swamy stared with pity at Freddy. Another example of a senior officer bending the rules to keep the boss happy in the PMO. He could bet the CDC had, with a wink and a smile, mentioned some attractive position in some overseas embassy.

"Freddy, my dear friend, I am waiting for an answer."

Freddy knew he had flouted the rules. He looked down at his shoes, realising that this was now stepping into the serious realm of disciplinary action.

"Sir, I am truly sorry. It's just that CDC was in some kind of panic. He made at least four calls to me the same morning of the debrief and impressed upon me that PMO was in need of the information asap. Coming from the PMO, I guess, I gave it some seriousness and decided to move ahead. I would have certainly input the query in the system later on. You do know, I have more than two decades in service, sir. I am not a child."

Swamy gently got up from the chair.

"Kaul, please record our meeting into the system. Please revoke Freddy's access rights for two weeks till I get to the bottom of this. I don't think I need to tell Akram what to do. He would have raised the security status in any case. Freddy, stay low, my friend. I am just being careful, nothing personal. Let's see where this goes. Of course, you are instructed not to engage with Project Chexo or the PMO office or the CDC. Should you get any call, please ensure to upload each recording onto the system. And Freddy, you are given a formal warning on record for breaking protocol."

Swamy got up and walked straight out of the room. He was worried. Reaching his room, he instructed his colleague.

"Get CDC on the secure line please."

Chief Defence Controller was a position created by the PMO two years back. Lt General Rajkumar Deshpande had just retired from the armed forces. Known to have close affiliations to the Prime Minister, not a single eyebrow was raised when he was announced as CDC. The CDC was the PMO interface for all interaction and info flow from the Defence and Intelligence establishments to the PMO.

His thoughts were interrupted by the loud ring on his secure line.

"Yes?"

"CDC on line. Sir, transferring."

Swamy took a deep breath. Why did he not like Deshpande?

"Hello Swamy ji," General Deshpande had an effeminate voice and almost like a whisper.

"Namaskar Rajkumar ji. How are you?"

"All well Swamy ji, I got worried when I was told you wanted to speak with me. How can I help?"

Swamy was guarded with his words.

"Haha. No no. Nothing serious. Just wanted to check if I can be of some help. Freddy was telling me you wanted some information on one of our projects."

There was complete silence on the line. Swamy guessed that CDC was shocked that Freddy had disclosed his request to Swamy. He was wondering how to respond. Swamy had learnt that sometimes a direct frontal attack was the best tactic to get the truth out. He could almost feel the CDC's brain churning to figure out how to react.

"Information? Aah... hmmm. Swamyji... I can't really recollect."

"Look General Sahib. You didn't think this would get our attention, did you? You do know you had to raise it with me and not steamroll Freddy for the information. You have a minute General, to tell me what interest you have in the project. The next call will be to the Principal Secretary, PMO.

"Swamy ji. Okay, I recall now. Our foreign minister has been having some meetings with his Chinese counterpart and a new deal is being worked out. Strategic twenty-year partnership. One of the tenets, I understand, is full disclosure and cessation of covert ops in each other's countries. As the Chinese have offered some amazing border dispute giveaways, we wanted to make the first move to set up transparency in the relationship. You do know the Chinese senior delegation is coming to town in thirty-five days. We plan to sign this deal. PMO wanted details of all operations around China and Freddy told me of Project Chexo. Hence guided by PMO, I was in a rush and asked him to help me. That's that. What's the big deal?"

Swamy was shocked at this information. A Chinese VIP visiting India in just a month and no mention to RAW. A twenty-year deal being thrashed out, he guessed, by the MEA. But why was the CDC tasked to get information on covert operations? This was just the tip of the iceberg.

Using his most official tone that he could muster, he spoke in a louder pitch to the CDC.

"General, I am surprised at this information. You have just updated me, after I had to almost snatch it out of you, with information that seems highly irregular. We are working out a deal with the Chinese and we have no knowledge of this? Can you tell me why the usual FEEP have not been initiated?

The 'Foreign Entity Engagement Protocols' were an official process of involving all stakeholders in the country in key decisions that were being taken with respect to any deals that India may plan to strike with a foreign entity. The aim was to ensure that during negotiations, the nation's best interests were taken care of. These covered the heads of government bodies on trade, defence and intelligence. Director General of RAW was a key member, as many times deals involved action or rather inaction against Indian assets overseas or even assets of foreign countries in India.

General Deshpande retorted like a bruised leopard.

"Swamyji, I guess maybe PMO doesn't trust you, after some of the failures we have had with China. We know of your stand on our relationship with China. We can continue to have an aggressive stand or decide to engage with them and seek a future together. By the way, I had an excellent meeting in Beijing last month with my counterpart. China is now very keen to work with us. Trade and defence are key. We want a 'no hidden agenda' environment. And that, frankly, Swamyji, with you is just so difficult. There is fear that you will always try to scuttle any dialogue and maybe that's why PMO wanted to get information without using FEEP. Now that you do know, you might as well take it up with PMO. Goodbye, Swamyji. And also, we agree with our Chinese colleagues that in the new era of Indo-China 20-year partnership, there is no place for covert or 'Dark' operations. So I guess, you will have less of that work to do, no?" saying that, the General disconnected the line.

Swamy held the receiver in his hand. He could still hear the staccato beeps of the line on the phone. His immediate reaction was of disappointment that the PMO had decided to take such a drastic step and keep FEEP away.

He decided to speak with Brigadier Atul Malhotra. Atul was a dear friend and someone Swamy trusted with his life. He headed the Military Intelligence Unit.

He heard a click on the other side.

"Atul?"

"Hey Swaaaammmiiiii..." The ever-playful Atul never left an opportunity to use the Malgudi Days 'Swamy' signature tune whenever he spoke with Swamy. They were friends from the academy days and Atul was three years Swamy's junior.

Swamy could visualise Atul smiling. He was so fond of him.

"Atul, *tere naam ka bhi sambar banau kya? Saale!*"

"Arre Boss, don't be upset. So nice to see your name pop up on my phone."

"Atul, am a little worried. Do you have any clue about the Chinese delegation coming in for a meeting in the next month or so?"

There was a pause on the phone.

"Chinese team? And the Head of RAW is calling a junior in MI to confirm? RK come on, aren't we too old for this. Please, let's play our game of full disclosure!"

Swamy smiled. Atul was just too sharp. A pity he was caught up in a bit of politics; he should have been CDC for the country.

"You caught me, Atul. You are so right. I was fishing. I forgot you aced the IQ scores in the academy! Yes, I was informed in a rather casual way by the CDC about some 20-year deal, but FEEP were not followed, so I had no clue. CDC was attempting to extract information about one of our projects in a rather covert manner by pumping Freddy's ego balloon."

"Boss, I have been working for two weeks on a plan called 'Managing Borders with reduced conflict status'. Now that you are sharing this, perhaps this is part of the overall 20-year deal. Sounds good, but what are we giving China in return is the question? I think, you would be worried. Maybe you've infiltrated some exciting area in the far east?"

"Atul, you know I can't confirm or deny that, my friend. But what you've just told me just confirms my fears. There is a transaction being worked on by the government on its own. FEEP stakeholders are not in the know. Obviously, as they feel FEEP may not support it. I was worried, but now I am close to a panic attack, Atul"

"Sir, your assessment is so right. Well, knowing you, I think the PMO will soon have to deal with a powerful adversary in RAW. If there's anything I can help with, do let me know."

"Thanks Atul. Let's catch up soon when you come to Delhi. Maybe we can schedule a review with NSA soon. Would love to catch up, and of course, dinner at my place."

"I would love that. Catch you soon. Bye sir."

R.K. Swamy was known to be the cool guy even under pressure. In RAW for over twenty years now, he could claim to have run some terrific operations. Having his own government run a 'covert' operation right under his nose was just unacceptable. That too, China! He ran several scenarios as he thought of the next steps. It was dangerous. He had learnt that the Chinese were a most formidable foe. The closer they came to you, the deeper would be the knife in your back.

CHAPTER 7
THE 20-YEAR DEAL

New Delhi
2015

The India Times carried a 100-word snippet on the tenth page two days later. Mysteriously worded with a title, 'A Twenty-year Betrayal to China?' The article quoted high level sources in the government and stated that apparently, the government, to win some trade favours has planned to give up several disputed positions India had maintained over the last many years. The article stated that the government had not responded to queries.

Director General RAW, R.K. Swamy was smirking at the article. RAW was not without influence. He smiled and looked forward to an exciting day in office. Even as he kept the newspaper down, his phone rang and he saw his office assistant's name pop up.

"Yes, Sanjeev, *bolo...*"

"Sir, quite a crazy day. Have had PMO, CDC, and even Akram chasing me to fix time for meetings with you. Can I block your time for today? In fact, CDC said he tried your phone twenty-six times, but could not get through."

"Sanjeev, refuse all meetings. You can tell them that I am a little under the weather and will come back tomorrow. Also, please inform them that my phone has some network issues so calls won't reach me. Call Akram and tell him that I said '*Anda kaccha hai*!"

A twenty-year deal with the Chinese without RAW clearance? No bloody way! With this mention in the media, Swamy had played a masterstroke. The drivers of this programme now were on the defensive. Let them sweat it out a bit.

He saw a name flashing on his personal phone. 'Haka Noodles'. His code for Akram Khan! This must be a real emergency. Akram Khan was possibly one rare operative that Swamy knew in RAW who was always two steps ahead of the game. One thing he loved about Akram was his devotion to his relationships. His team trusted him blindly. He would integrate his family with his team's families, making it a strong bond. In a business where trust was in short supply, Akram Khan would always be a treasured asset.

"*Akram, tu theek hai na?*"

"Sir, got your message loud and clear. I had our asset in Beijing dig up information in the last 24 hours. There are celebrations all over in offices. This twenty-year deal had three core contours. Am sending you a picture. Take a look."

Swamy's phone buzzed and he opened the message. The picture was clearly a little fuzzy, taken from phone camera with some handshake.

- *Border retreat: India to retreat from established positions by 10 kms across the entire border. China promises not to redraw maps but just change current disputed territories. Media news will be fed with information of a so-called Moratorium on border dispute for 20 years*

- *Tibet solution: India will ban any further flow from Chinese occupied Tibet to India. The current Tibetan population to be relocated to Andaman and Nicobar Islands for a 20 year limited visa post which exile conditions will change and will require Tibetans to be deported to China.*
- *Transparency in Covert Ops: Both India and China to withdraw assets and also release list of locals enrolled in programmes so they can be neutralised by soft exits (meaning they will not be killed but asked to leave the country).*

In return, India will receive a Trade Deal incentive. Currently, India's Import from China were approx. 60 Bn$ and exports were only 16 bn$. A 44 Bn $ deficit. China proposed that for 20 years, it will underwrite an import by China value of $ 118. This would therefore be the value of Indian exports guaranteed by China. This would be possible, for as long as India continued to import a value of 18 Bn and the ratio stayed unchanged. This was an incredible deal for India and the government could easily use this as a significant job generator initiative. It could be an excellent election card. Peace and money! As Akram was summarising all this, Swamy could not help but be impressed with what Project Chexo had achieved. Akram had done an incredible job. To manage to get this information within 48 hours was in itself very impressive.

"Akram, this is good. Leave it with me. Please do not change your risk status. I will keep you updated."

Akram pondered over these words. He was being told by the Head of RAW to maintain the risk status he had changed in a fit of anger. This 20-year deal was ridiculous. The discussion on covert operations was like a death sentence for his operation.

Swamy continued, "And Akram, you will be notified by the Personnel department. You have taken copy book steps in your engagement with the two Spocs. Please continue to have zero engagement with any other government entity. Please stop all communication and go into Eclipse mode for forty-eight hours."

"Copy, Chief. Thanks."

Eclipse mode was when all information flow from an operation is stopped from leaving the project's premises. All e-mails are blocked, all phone lines, web access and so on go into silent mode.

A storm was brewing.

***

R.K. Swamy's house unit on Akbar Road was spread over almost 4000 square yards in central Delhi. His two Indie dogs Luka and Luna, adopted a year back were his de-stress package. Sitting in his lawn with a cup of his favourite Kangra tea, he was amazed at how well the household had taken to his canine companions. His wife, Vedica and he lived alone in this shamefully huge house. Five bedrooms and an incredible lawn looked after by a team of seven staff members, it was almost embarrassing for just a couple and two dogs to live in such an enormous property. Vedica and he had never had any children. They did try for a number of years, but finally, they both gave up. He focused on his career and Vedica on her role at a special needs primary school. Vedica was very fond of Akram's daughter and they had developed a strong bond over the years.

Luka and Luna were chasing squirrels and peacocks in the garden. It was almost 6.45 a.m. and he knew he had a tough day ahead of him. The tragedy of Democracy was that sometimes the greed for power led even the most honest to think of surreptitious ways to stay in office. Of course, he understood the need to win votes, but at the cost of betraying your country was alarming. This was no less than betrayal. As Swamy felt anger well up, he stopped that thought and shouted across,

"Luka... Luna! Come on boys... biscuits..."

The dogs reacted with agility and sprinted to Swamy, jumping onto him for their favourite treats. As Swamy gave in and handed out their biscuits, he heard his phone message buzzer go off.

His assistant Sanjeev had messaged –

Sir, urgent meeting Principal Secretary to PM, Surinder Singh and CDC @11 am @PMO. Security Protocol initiated.

All meetings in PMO required a special protocol. Specially, if the meeting had more than 2 'People of Interest' (POI). POIs were the Indian government's top fifty individuals who had the highest level of security clearance. As three of them were part of the list, a special security procedure was required to ensure the security of the individuals as well as the location.

Swamy took a deep breath. Here goes, he thought to himself.

As the DG, RAW's car turned into the PMO, the security personnel were at his door even before the car stopped. His personal security consisted of six RAW Personnel Department

'Administration' staff. RAW did not allow any external security agency access to its personnel. About twenty years back, a small incident of infiltration caused the death of two of RAW's middle layer officers. Since then, RAW had developed its own personnel security unit consisting of 180 specially trained and equipped teams. They were trained in Myanmar at a special site run by the government. This allowed RAW to use foreign trainers as well. The training campus was headed by an ex-SAS (British special forces) Major.

Even before anyone could touch his car's door handle, Swamy's team had taken the first perimeter security of the Director. Even the black cat commandoes in the PMO were not allowed in this first perimeter.

Swamy was not looking forward to this meeting. He could already guess that the outcome wouldn't be pleasant. He had already been branded as anti-China and that's why the FEEP process had not been adhered to. A pity that the government did not trust him enough to confide in him. He knew that he must resign in protest, at this point. This would not have a happy ending, and he didn't want to be near this.

Swamy was ushered into the main boardroom at the PMO. The CDC was already in the room. Swamy nodded at him with a cold smile. General Deshpande looked sullen. He gave a cold nod and continued to stare at the table. Swamy never did like men who avoided eye contact. I don't trust you one bit, Deshpande.

Gloved service team came in and glasses of water with the standard government issue cookies were kept on the table. Swamy requested for a coffee and the CDC refused to order anything.

Principal Secretary Surinder Singh walked in with his assistant who would take notes. As soon as he sat down, Surinder Singh dismissed his assistant

“You carry on, Raju. We won’t need your help. This meeting will not be minuted. Please also ensure meeting record is not entered in the booking diary.”

Surinder looked at Swamy and held his hand out.

“Hi stranger! Long time!”

Swamy shook his hand. He had interacted with Surinder several times. He knew that the PM was really fond of him. In fact, Surinder had superseded several senior civil servants to be appointed to the, possibly, most important civil servant job in India.

“Indeed long time, Surinder.”

Surinder glanced at the CDC.

“Hi General sahib. Should we start?”

The CDC looked back and nodded.

“Okay, Swamy, so the PM has cleared me to pull you into a new deal in the making with China. CDC has briefed me about his discussion with you and am quite willing to admit that the CDC using such clandestine methods to get information were unwarranted and totally unacceptable. We all know the history between you two, so I am willing to write this off as a bad choice by the CDC.”

Swamy could see the CDC turning ashen at this reprimand. But what was he expecting? PMO to agree that they asked him to find info like this? No way!

"Anyhow, PM has asked me to personally brief you Swamy, so the CDC and you can now work on this together. A month back, Himachal Pradesh local police arrested a foreign national who claimed to be Tibetan, in Dharamsala. He was arrested from a hotel in the local market Kotwali Bazaar. As it turns out, the local hotel staff overheard him talking to a few locals in his room. He was discussing how to collect some travel details of His Holiness the Dalia Lama. The hotel staff was a young man, who we think was a keen movie buff. He smelt a conspiracy and decided to put his mobile phone camera in a flower pot in the room with a timer. He managed to figure out when this person would get the local folks into the room and he decided to record them. The first recording itself was incredible. This chap spoke in Lhasa dialect of Tibetan. The summary of this was that he was offering USD 50,000 in cash to get the detailed travel plans of His Holiness. Things get murky because once he found a local who was willing to help, he then offered another 50k USD to the local to give him entrance details to the monastery and the food habits of the Dalai Lama."

Swamy was listening with full attention.

"On getting some locals to interpret the dialect in the video, the local police swung into action. They arrested him. They had some 'persuasive discussions' and the chap confessed that he was a part of the Strategic Huyou Agency (SHA) in the Ministry of State Security, China. He was inserted into India from Nepal six months back, without any travel documents. His mission was to find ways and means to assassinate the Dalai Lama and make it look like poisoning or a car accident."

Surinder was looking straight at Swamy. He knew they needed Swamy on their side now.

"MEA invited the Chinese ambassador and the video clips were shown to them. To cut to the chase, China wants to bury this and is willing to have a deal. MEA and PMO have been hammering out the deal, contours of which are not even documented yet."

Swamy had a career of meeting folks who were good at being spin doctors. He knew something was amiss. Surinder was looking at him now, waiting for a reaction.

Swamy without breaking eye contact, extracted a printed page from his satchel and handed it to Surinder.

"Surinder, here are the contours of the deal as documented by your office to the Chinese Ambassador. This document is straight from the files in the specific unit who is 'hammering out the details'. I especially like the trade wins and the retreat from the border. CDC too must have cleared it. Does the Army Chief know? Am wondering why hasn't the FEEP been initiated yet. Sir, do you mind telling what me the hell is happening? Foreign agents are arrested in Dharamsala and not a word to my office? Surinder, I can spot a fairytale and I can tell you, this spin is full of shit!"

Swamy was just getting started

"Someone asked the Military Intelligence to prepare a plan with drastic reduction in forces on the border. Oh really! You guys have no idea of the Chinese. I can understand you don't trust me, Surinder. So I think it's best we think of my exit. What are you doing is plain and simple treachery and it won't be allowed on my watch. You spin some hogwash about catching a Chinese agent in Dharamsala. Sorry, Surinder, let me tell you, you guys want the trade deal and that's that. You are willing to go to any length for this. What the hell is 'transparency in covert ops'. These ops are *my* ops, Surinder Singh. Indians who have put their lives at stake."

There was deathly silence in the room.

RAW had access to the deal contours. That too from China! Surinder and the CDC's jaws dropped to the floor.

Surinder abruptly got up and walked out of the room.

Swamy thought to himself. Looks like the PM is getting an urgent update.

Almost eighteen minutes passed. The CDC and Swamy had a tough time just waiting. Just when Swamy thought that he would leave, the door opened and Surinder walked back in.

He gestured to the CDC, "Some privacy please, General!"

CDC made a strange grunt and walked straight out of the room.

Surinder glared at Swamy.

"Just had a chat with the PM, Swamy. Let me give you some clear messages here. First, information that you have is not accurate at all. Moreover, how do you know your asset isn't playing a double game? Perhaps an attempt to create some trust deficit in the ranks of the government, eh? You are a seasoned player. How can you trust this document? We are still to close out all aspects of the deal. Which is why you have been summoned here today, Swamy. You need to stop playing these double games here.

"What is clear is that while we figure the deal out, we have agreed with the Chinese counterpart to cease and desist all covert operations against each other. China has already given us a list and those assets are being exited from India. As a counter, we too have promised the same. So, you are instructed to update the PM on detailed list of assets and locally recruited assets so they may be given safe passage back to India. Do you understand, Swamy?"

"Surinder, are you smoking something? Are you totally mad? Do you know each asset builds a local group? Each asset will have eight to ten local assets. As soon as we blow the cover of these assets, the local assets will get exposed. We may get safe exit, but what about the local assets? What do you think the Chinese government will do to them? Give them a fucking award! Surinder, you want to shut down operations, no problem. We will exit all assets over the next six months. It will be all very quiet and that's that. Do *you* understand, Surinder?"

"Swamy, no. China gave us a list and so will we."

"List, what bloody list? How many operatives are there? Tell me."

"Ummm, about twenty, mostly in Dharamsala."

"You idiot, they are giving you fake names of Tibetans in India. Will China ever reveal names of their assets? Are you absolutely mad?" Swamy was shouting and had stood up towering over Surinder.

Surinder was in shock. "Swamy, get out! We will speak later."

Swamy continued.

"Surinder, you guys have crossed the line. Doing such deals without FEEP is treason. Looks like you are willing to do anything for the trade dollars. I will not allow this, Surinder. Over my dead body!"

Swamy got up and marched right out of the meeting room.

His RAW team sprang into action as he nodded to the team leader. Surinder came out of the room.

"Swamy, this is not acceptable. Come back and we need to discuss this... *Swamy*!" Surinder was walking fast just behind Swamy.

Swamy stopped in his tracks, turned around and glared at Surinder.

"Surinder, you've sold your soul. I am disappointed with what you guys are doing. You've wanted me out of the picture, right? Yes? You will get it. But, not before I make sure this nation is safe."

Swamy moved closer to Surinder putting his face right next to his ear. "Surinder, you are putting our country at grave risk. Wake up!"

With this Swamy turned and left a shocked Surinder in the corridors of the PMO.

The RAW protection team leader had already messaged the convoy and by the time the team stepped out, the vehicles had already reached the porch. Swamy was still shaking his head in anger and mumbling to himself. Getting into his car, Swamy barked to his driver.

"*Ghar chalo,* Pramod!"

It was rare but the DG, RAW was furious.

Akram Khan. Swamy was thinking of him. In all this madness, he could not help but admire the RAW trained officer. Incredible, the country will never be able to appreciate what he had set up. He knew he had to put things into motion. Was the government the enemy now? He could not but start processing the many scenarios. Like a game of chess, he had to think of the next five moves the other side could take. In all of these, Swamy noted, that Akram would face disaster either way. He felt terrible. He took a deep breath and planned his next move. Akram, my friend, we need you. We need you now, like never before.

***

Akram Khan was planning his own next moves. Swamy had been his key mentor. He could sense what was happening. As he sat in his living room, staring at this garden outside, his gaze shifted to his favourite family picture in the corridor just next to him. It was a black and white photograph with the paper already turned a light yellow with age. There were two young men in white baggy trousers, standing rather straight with nervous smiles and a pretty smart young woman sitting in between them. Behind them he could see a shop with a small signboard on top that read 'Ekla Café'. All three looked formal, posing for the photograph. Just under the photograph was a handwritten note in beautiful handwriting. The note read 'Friends for freedom. December 1912'. He sighed at the picture and recalled the amazing history he was part of that included, if you please, a Hindu Bengali great grandfather! He could faintly recall his grandmother narrating tales of the freedom struggle. The families were still in touch . Prabal's line had set up a chain of Ekla Cafes that the great grandchildren now looked after. The real treasure was, of course, with his grandmother in Kolkatta. A travel case full of memorabilia. Ah! It had been sometime he had been to Kolkatta. He looked at the photograph and a smile played on his lips, full of pride of his ancestry.

CHAPTER 8
TREASON

Calcutta
1912

An excited child greeted Prabal when he entered his café at 8 a.m. sharp. The café opened at 7.18 a.m. and he liked to be there early. Prodipto, who loved the aroma of freshly baked bread, was already at his favourite table near the rear door that led to the bakery.

"Aha, Prabal, owner decides to come late. Eh?"

Prodipto was sitting with Pavitra and he could see both of them grinning from ear to ear. He didn't really like Pavitra getting involved with the Anushilan Samiti, but she was Pavitra. Her passion for a free India was incredible and so very sharp. He was proud of her, but also feared for her safety. After the British had arrested the Ghosh brothers and eight others, he was always worried if they would pick his scent as well.

Prabal sat down and yelled out for a chai with a vanilla cookie.

"Have the two of you won some lottery or something? Or have you finally agreed to get married?"

He loved to tease them. He knew there was some romance lurking here and he would be only too happy for Pavitra. Prodipto was his closest friend. He did worry though that he was putting him in harm's way.

Pavitra froze with the comment and just looked away and Prodipto blushed a deep red! Prabal just loved the reaction and burst out laughing.

"Okay... okay, so what's happening here to get the world famous architect to our café in the morning?"

"Prabal, I've cracked it. I know how to build that tunnel," Prodipto was almost shouting.

Prabal asked him to lower his voice with a quick gesture.

"Shhh... pipe down... What are you saying?"

"I don't need to build it. I will get the British Architecture Department to design it for us and they will also build it for us, free of cost."

Prabal took all this in and was sure that Prodipto had just lost it.

"Hey hey! What are you saying? Slow down! You mean the tunnel under the Viceroy House will be built by the British government at their own cost so we can use it? Well you know what, you are crazy! What nonsense is this?"

"Just listen to me, Prabal. Do you know what a king's escape is?"

"No, what the hell is that?"

"In Europe, all royalty had a special escape route built in their castles, mansions, and so on. In case of a revolt, attack or an assassination attempt, they would use this route to escape. In design language, it was always branded as 'king's escape'. I took a special course in it as it was remarkable."

While Prodipto chatted on like a kid with a new toy, Prabal could see Pavitra watching Prodipto, with awe and pride. God, she loves him! Prabal thought to himself.

"So, Prodipto, how does this history lesson help us?" Prabal interrupted the gleeful chatter of his friend.

"Prabal, don't you see? I am going to design a king's escape. I will record to Lutyens that Mr Baker is designing it and I will tell Mr Baker that Lutyens has been given charge of this. They don't talk to each other, so they will never guess. There's so much in fighting that my guess is they will just leave it there. Once it's in the plans with specific structure details, the British engineers will just construct it and no one will ever know! Isn't it brilliant? It's just incredible. A secret tunnel designed by yours truly constructed by the British and always part of the history of this land."

Prabal was astounded. If what Prodipto was saying was possible, it would be incredible. This guy was a genius. There was no stopping his friend now. He continued to chatter about the plans.

"In fact, I am going to use some amazing new material for the structure. Let's see – we need to take it at least fifteen feet underground and a slope with cobbled stones for horses to easily gallop through. Hmm, and we will prepare for sources of light. I will need concealed exits and several points. Where should I exit in the Viceroy House? Hmm... I will have to think of that. Of course, we will put the layout in the drafts in a manner no one can simply just locate it. How do I design the exits? It will need some innovative structures!"

"Dada, hold it, my young excited child. I have some questions for you. You do recall there is a purpose to build the tunnel. This isn't a historic monument you are building. We don't want something so complex that takes twenty years to build. When do you think it will be ready? Can we live inside the tunnel for a week or so? We need to plan the exits. Whatever we are planning, we may not have too much time before the alarms go off."

Prodipto broke his chain of thought. As usual, his astute planner was right.

"Yes, Prabal. You are right, my design training took over. I understand what you are saying. I will sneak out the last available design and go over the position of the exits with you. Yes, we will have a 'life sustainable' tunnel that will have air circulation pathways. I will build latrines as well. Enough so we can live there for seven days. How long it will take? See the tunnel will have to be made before the overhead construct. I think it may take two to three years."

This is too long, Prabal thought to himself. We won't have so many years of patience. With the extensive network of *khabris, the* British might just stumble upon their plan and they may have to escape to Japan even before they could use the tunnel.

"Prodipto, can you somehow get an operational tunnel so that we can use it even before the full overhead structure is ready? The Viceroy will inspect it once a year at least. If this event can happen right inside the Viceroy House, even if it is not completely ready, it will be a fantastic achievement."

"Hmmm... aren't you getting demanding now? Do you understand how complex this is? You want a tunnel tomorrow morning? Ridiculous!"

Prabal sensed the frustration. He had to manage this child carefully. He glanced at Pavitra and she knew what he wanted.

She spoke in a whisper.

"I think, won't it be amazing that an Indian architect designs a world class tunnel to get India freedom." She looked at Prodipto, seeking a response.

Prodipto took the bait.

"Hmm.... yes yes... Let me work something out. I must get going. Lot of work to be done. By the way, what happens post the event? You don't think the British will just walk away. We know what happened in the five years after 1857, don't we?"

"Don't worry, my genius architect," Prabal took his hand. "Plans already in the works. You do know that the French and the Japanese are our supporters. Why do you think Harobindo Ghosh went to Pondicherry? Huh? In fact, the French are sending one of their best to help Auro set up a training station in Pondicherry. Weapons and bombs. The French also have some Turks helping them on the explosives design. For us, the safe passage will be to Japan. Immediately after the event, eighteen of us will leave for Japan. We can even take your jiji with us."

Prodipto pondered over this. He had never thought of the aftermath. Japan? What about his practice. His jiji. Japan. He stared at Prabal.

"I know what you are thinking, my friend," Prabal spoke up. "It's only for a few years. Once we get independence, we will come back to a heroes' welcome."

He pulled Prodipto's cheeks and was glad to see him smile. Prabal knew that there was a high chance that they may be arrested by the British. He needed to make sure Pavitra and Prodipto made it out.

Prodipto nodded and got up. He hugged Prabal and nodded to Pavitra.

"What... no hug for me?" Pavitra teased Prodipto and was amused to see him blush and run out of the café.

It was almost 9.18 a.m. Prodipto decided to head straight to the office. His mind was racing in several directions.

He knew he had to involve Richard. Richard had to sign off the designs. He knew how this had to work. He knew Richard admired Herbert Baker more than Lutyens.

Entering his office, he took out the last draft with the comments of both Baker and Lutyens. He noted on the bottom right corner, Herbert Baker's comment. Taking a pencil with similar colour gauge, he studied Baker's handwriting flow and placed the following just under the comment

I insist on the King's escape. Has to be underground with a good 1 km exit from the VH.

He studied his forgery and was quite impressed with the output. Hmm... am good at this, he thought. It had taken him a good one hour to perfect it. He used a light sandpaper to make it look a little aged. He rolled up the draft and walked straight to Richard's office.

He could see Richard working on the draft table.

"May I enter, sir?"

"Of course, my young friend. So you are still calling me 'sir' eh? You're just plain feeble minded, my dear sir. Come in come in."

"Richard, I wanted to just show you one of the designs of the corridor pillars in the two blocks outside the VH. I think we need something more here. Wanted your views."

Prodipto knew Richard loved the design part of the work. The pillar design comments had several comments from Baker and Prodipto planned to just let Richard discover the comment on the King's escape. The idea had to come from Richard.

"You do know, Prodipto, that the design committee has, for the sake of peace, carved out the work schedules for Lutyens and Baker. So Lutyens will design the VH and the entire 400 metre radius around the VH. Baker will design the two office blocks outside the VH as well as the area outside the 400-metre perimeter."

Prodipto was delighted with this news. So Baker would develop the area around the VH. The exit of the tunnel would come under Baker's designs!

Prodipto unrolled he canvas, clipping it to the edges of the table. He pointed to the pillar head design and pointed it to Richard.

"This one sir. Isn't the top looking too plain?"

Richard came closer to the canvas, adjusting his glasses. He carefully went over the pillar top, took out his drafting pencil and in less than a minute had recrafted the top. He had given it a 'jali' design on the top. Prodipto smiled. Richard was impressive. He had clearly seen these in the Kali temple designs in Calcutta and used a very Indian motif.

"Aha, that's beautiful, sir, and in less than a minute."

"Does look nice, eh? I think Mr Baker will like it, eh? Hold on, what has he scribbled just on the bottom of the pillar head. I may have missed it."

He came closer to the canvas and Prodipto felt his heart starting to race. He could not help but comment in all innocence.

"Oh, I didn't really give it much attention. I think it was about the pillar head design... and I couldn't even understand. Something about the King—"

He waited for a reaction from Richard. There was a ten second silence that seemed like hours to Prodipto.

"What does it say, Richard?"

Richard stepped back and looked straight and hard at Prodipto.

"Prodipto, I have delegated a lot of work to you. Specially the listing of all comments by our two chief designers. Do you bloody know what a blunder you have done? Baker is brilliant. Even Lutyens didn't think of this. That's why I admire him. Oh god! What a blunder not to have Baker design the VH and give it to this country home designer Lutyens. No one thought of this. He wants a bloody king's escape. Why didn't I think of this? The Viceroy too is at risk. Specially now with the growth of terrorists. Brilliant, Mr Baker! Brilliant!"

Richard was clapping and enjoying his Eureka moment.

Prodipto was staring at Richard. This was going far better than he anticipated.

"King's escape... Oh, that word is 'escape', it looked like 'cape' to me so I could not understand."

"Yes, yes, Prodipto. This is exciting. I haven't designed one in ages. Did you do this elective in your programme?"

"In fact, sir, I did. And now I am recalling the programme. Aha, so Mr Baker wants to make a passage for the Viceroy."

"Great, so you can help as well. Come, now leave me be and I will give you a draft design tomorrow. Let me see where it will best fit in our current designs."

"Sure, Richard sir."

"I knew it in my bones. Baker is a genius. A king's escape! Amazing. He is so bloody sharp. How could we miss this?"

Richard asked him to go away with a dismissive wave of his hand, still mumbling to himself.

As Prodipto walked away, he felt a tad guilty of using Richard. He thought, Richard loved India as much as any Indian. Am sure he wouldn't mind contributing to India's freedom. He had an immense sense of achievement in what had been triggered. He had just put the tunnel into the hands of the Chief Architect in India. God save the queen! He was just thinking to himself if Richard could be accused of helping terrorists. His thoughts were interrupted as he entered his room.

Bullu was waiting for him in his room.

"Sahib, Prabal sir calling you to Ekla."

Now what was up?

Prodipto rushed to Ekla Café, only to find Prabal and Pavitra helping serve clients.

"Hey young genius, glad you could make it. Look what my friends from France sent me."

He stood aside and Prodipto saw a black box on top of a long three-legged frame.

"It's a bloody expensive thing, eh? A picture-taking camera. Yes, just off the production line.

"Come, come. I thought that the first picture has to be with two of my favourite people. I have already trained Basudev on it." Basudev was Ekla café's accountant.

Soon, Prabal, Prodipto and Pavitra were posing in front of the camera. Basudev worked on the camera. He yelled, "Clicking 1, clicking 2 and clicking..."

Click went the camera with a loud shutter sound. Little did Prodipto know, this picture would be part of his legacy for his great grandson Akram Khan.

CHAPTER 9
BETRAYAL

India –China
2010-2015

Chinpa Drolma aka, Yu Yan, lived in Lhasa Tibet. Just behind Jiangsu Avenue in the Chengguan District. Yu Yan was her chosen name that she had taken on four years ago when she moved from Dharamsala to China. The nature of her employment did not allow formal routes of transport. Armed with her forged documents, she had crossed the border from Bhutan.

Chinpa was her given name. She had little recollection of her parents. Her mother passed away the moment she was born and her father fell prey to drug addiction and died of an overdose in the hospital in Dharamsala where she was born. She was then, at the age of seven, moved out to an orphanage just above Mcleodganj. Mcleodganj was the relocation centre of all Tibetans when they moved to India. A small town just above Kangra valley, it had become mini Tibet over the years. Yu Yan was recruit number 17 of Project Chexo. Her handler, Chen, was a fellow Tibetan who was around forty-five years old. In the last four years, she had made four trips back to Dharamsala. That, for her, was the closest thing to home. She was picked up at age of sixteen by Chen and inducted into the team. For her, this was an incredible break. She had only heard of Tibet from friends. It was her real home.

She discovered that Chen had some links to the Indian government. He was staying at a small one-bedroom accommodation near Triund lake much above Mcleodganj. Just behind his small cottage was a large field of approximately 4000 sq yards that was built like a road obstacle course. Chinpa was persuaded by Chen to join the group that would be sent to Tibet to stay there. The Indian government would help them to build a life there. She knew then that there was something more to this. She met about eleven other Tibetans from all over the country who had also enrolled with Chen. They were given bunk beds in a hall next to the sports field. For two years they trained in Mcleodganj, living in the hall and being trained by Chen. It was a good life. They had high quality food and access to a large TV screen. It included free time of three hours every day and occasional trips to Kotwali bazaar for their famous ice cream! They also spent four hours a day on academic studies, studying science and biology. Chinpa had not really thought much before enrolling. She liked Chen and he was the only father figure she had had in her life. She was in awe of his fitness level, his command over English, Hindi as well as the Lhasa dialect of Chinese. Often, she would notice army jeeps, cars with government flags picking up Chen, following which he would disappear for hours.

On her eighteenth birthday, Chen took her out for a lavish meal to Noodle Soup House near the monastery. Then they went to the monastery to offer prayers, followed by a walk on the conical forest lanes. She had a vivid memory of that discussion. Chen shared with her that she was now an adult. He shared information about her father, whom she had never known. How he was an activist for the Tibetan 'Free Tibet' movement. He went on to share that Tibetans owed a great deal to India. Slowly, he unveiled the real reasons why she was taken under his wings.

"Chinpa, I work for the Government of India. I am part of a project where Tibetans are trained and sent to Tibet to gather information to help us Tibetans as well as the Indian government. We are alive due to the generosity of the Indian government. Many of our brothers and sisters have been killed by the Chinese. We must get regular information about them. Now, do you realise what a fantastic opportunity faces you? You can help your people, help India and help us repay this debt we have to Indians."

Chinpa took all this in. She could not think of even saying no. What else would she do in India? Chen was the only family she had. She nodded. Chen enveloped her in a bear hug and when he released her, they both had tears rolling down their cheeks.

Chen took her hand, "You are special, Chinpa. Your fitness levels are amazing and your grasp of physics and biology unique. Of our lot, three are being chosen for this project. You are lucky and I am so happy you have accepted."

She just looked down. She was not used to being praised like this.

"So what next for me, Chen?"

"Honey, you and three others will leave this coming Sunday for Delhi via the airport at Gaggal near Dharamsala. You will be headed to New Delhi where you will stay for three months. More training, I am afraid, but now this will be specialised training. Then you will be off to Myanmar where we have a special school for talented folks like you."

Chen was talking of the RAW training centre in Myanmar.

The next year went by like a blur. Myanmar was an amazing experience and the RAW training facility seemed to be out of the future. The team of four that she was part of went through almost nine months of incredible training. Her first class in 'Human Anatomy' combined ancient defence techniques from Kerala in India as well as Japanese techniques. Daze, Immobilise and Neutralise were the only three options. Human fingers were the most potent weapons for close armed combat. Hand to hand, weapons, technology, explosives as well as using advanced monitoring equipment were an integral part of the training. In addition, special language courses had started in Dharamsala itself that helped them learn and speak the Tibetan dialect of Chinese.

Chinpa's background profile or 'Insertion Background and Documentation (IBD)' was a complete department in RAW. Right from birth documents to her Chinese parents' family album, everything was built by this team. She had a 'mentor' in Tibet who would help her get started for six months and then go back to his base location in China.

On at least four occasions, she met some Indians as well. Chen stayed for about a month and it was great to spend time with someone who she considered as close to a father as she could imagine.

The head of the facility in Myanmar was headed by a white guy who she would often see in the mess. There were regular history lessons as well on how Indians were the saviours for the Tibetans, etc, etc. She didn't need any convincing, though. She hated the Chinese and that convinced her whose side she was on.

Once implanted in Tibet, Yu Yan worked in the local kitchen catering to the police training academy. The position was created when the previous helper was accidentally run over by a truck in the evening while walking back home. Yu Yan's mentor dumped the truck in a lake close by. Sometimes tough decisions had to be taken to progress towards one's target. Yu Yan was placed after some money exchanged hands, and after a month, Yu Yan was on her own.

She made friends quickly, rented a small apartment and also offered a co-worker to live with her for free. It was a smart move as it was another source of information. So far, Yu Yan had not been given any explicit instructions about creating her own network. She was to be in touch every three months. Her life had soon settled into a pattern. Compared to India, Yu Yan noticed the difference. Everything had a rule and fear was palpable. The government had informers all around and one had to be extremely careful. But she noticed that things worked. There was a system for everything and it worked well.

She had made several friends with her co-workers. Initially, in spite of her training, the language was a challenge. The dialect was somewhat different and often friends remarked, which Yu Yan laughed off.

That evening Yu Yan had promised to cook for her friends and taken permission to leave an hour early. As the clock struck four in the afternoon, she finished her last chore of peeling the potatoes for the next day. She stored them, took her bag and yelled to the floor, saying a quick bye.

Yu Yan was thinking of her recipe for that night's dinner. As she walked towards her apartment, she knew she would need to do something with pork. She loved pork. When you are part on an insertion, it took just a year to dull you into thinking that this was normal. The challenge being that there can't be a mock drill of when you are part of a 'merge with population' process. Yu Yan always knew that, but yet, in just two years, she had begun to like her life here. Everything worked to the clock and the sense of normalcy sometimes made her forget her real identity. She was thinking of pork and her thoughts just drifted to Chen, who would make the most delicious pork chops in Dharamsala. Chen, I do miss you. She had just reached her apartment and was turning towards her door, when she saw a smiling young girl at the footsteps of her staircase. Yu Yan smiled back thinking she must be a new neighbour.

As she approached the staircase, the young girl dressed in smart black trousers and a white top made a slight bow and said,

"Hei, Yu Yan."

Yu Yan was startled. Was she someone from the kitchen?

She bowed back in greeting and that was a terrible mistake.

The moment Yu Yan bowed, the other girl used a sudden move. Using her right hand, she delivered a forceful blow to Yu Yan's side of the neck on the jugular. This stunned Yu Yan and before she could react, the second blow knocked her cold. Before she hit the floor, she saw that the visitor had stopped smiling.

"Or should we say Ms Chinpa from India. Sorry, darling, all for your own good, trust me!"

A black BMW car drove right to the front. Two young men jumped out and picked up Yu Yan and bundled her into the car. Another car drove in and five men burst out. Climbing the staircase, they raced up to Yu Yan's room. They knew what had to be done.

China knew.

CHAPTER 10
TRAITOR

New Delhi
2015

Akram Khan woke up with a start. He was a sound sleeper, but he was trained to pick out any out-of-the-ordinary ambient noises. He knew his senses had picked something sending an alarm through his system. Aarti was in deep sleep and he could hear her light breathing. The bedroom had a night light near the door. Akram had chosen to stay with his mother in their heritage house on Hanuman Road near Connaught Place. His mother refused to leave the house, so Akram had refused the government accommodation.

Straining to pick up any sounds, Akram swiftly got up. Walking out of the bedroom slowly, he chose not to wear his slippers. His bedroom was on the first floor. He decided to check the living room area, but as soon as he moved to the staircase, he heard a loud click from the kitchen. He turned towards the kitchen and swiftly moved to the main door of the kitchen. The kitchen had access from a rear door that allowed the staff to enter the kitchen on the ground floor as well as the first floor. As the staff had an entrance from the rear door of the house, Akram could already guess how the intruder had got in.

The kitchen door had a round see through window and Akram stood right next to the door. He strained to pick up movement. He realised he had left his phone on his bedside and protocol demanded that he speed dialled 001. All RAW staff had emergency protocols. A quick speed dial triggered an emergency response. As the staff dealt with situations where they could be kidnapped and tortured for information, there were effective systems set up to help staff in case of any emergency.

Akram decided to rush in and neutralise any threat. His mother, daughter and wife were in the house and he wasn't taking chances.

Just as Akram pumped himself up, bracing himself to rush in, he froze as he heard a voice from the kitchen.

"Mr Khan, you are getting old..."

Akram was shocked as he heard Samdup's voice. The door swung open with Samdup standing right outside.

Akram was in shock at Samdup's entry.

"What the bloody hell, you idiot? What if I had used my Glock? Are you mad, pulling this kind of a stunt? Why didn't you call me or use the front door bell?"

Akram could sense his breathing slowing down as relief calmed his nerves. He was still in shock.

"Sorry, boss. Something's amiss. I think your phone is on tap since the last five days. I am also suspecting that your house is being watched. So, had to make an entry from the kitchen."

"Sammy, are you mad? My phone on tap? Are you crazy? You know all are our phones have security apps that will set off an alarm. And what the hell were you doing for the last six minutes? I woke up seven minutes back, so you were in the kitchen and then it took you six minutes to spot me."

"Aaaah... Mr Khan, sharp as usual. Well I did get into the kitchen almost twenty-five minutes back. I think I shut the refrigerator door with a bit of a bang."

"What... twenty-five minutes back?"

"Hold on, a man gets hungry, right? Was planning to softly wake you up by knocking on your bedroom door. I had all the time in the world, so decided to finish off the leftovers. Yellow dal and bread is delicious, no?"

Akram looked at his friend and could not help smiling.

"I almost had a heart attack. I am getting old for this shit, man!"

"Yes boss. You are. You stood next to the kitchen door not realising there is a wall mirror just behind you. I could see you clearly through the kitchen door see through glass. Tsk Tsk, poor...very poor. You're getting old, Mr Khan."

Akram pulled Samdup for a hug and they both walked into the family lounge. Akram's daughter and his mother used the bedroom on the ground floor.

Samdup rushed to draw the curtains and then flipped on the light.

"Akram, something's going on. I am worried. I realised this evening and in fact Kyle noticed that our data back up unit in office had two guys going ghost on us in the last six days."

Project Chexo's data system's unit had almost six sharp tech whizzes to deal with data. Every meeting and document that came through the system was logged. Optical character recognition (OCR) technology helped index every scanned document as well. Voice recordings of meetings were transcribed into document files that were then indexed.

"What do you mean?"

"Kyle called me in the afternoon to say that our AI system tracker raised a red flag."

The Artificial Intelligence tracker analysed all the data with all employees of Project Chexo to throw up any event or action that was out of the ordinary.

"He told me that the system identified that two new computer access ids and passwords were generated for two new assignees in the span of four days. This was quite strange. The data unit was set up with the help of NIA's National Datamatics Unit. Only employees who had security clearances could be assigned to RAW projects. Kyle went into the details, he found it even more strange. Both the employees that had stopped coming to work were employees who stayed in the same apartment complex and also had a common source hometown."

Akram was watching Samdup and he felt bile coming up his throat. Anxiety often did this to him.

"Kyle called both the numbers of the new employees, but they were switched off. He tracked the GPS and for the last three days, there was no movement. He sent a scout. Both stayed alone and there was no one at their homes. The scout broke into the homes and everything was there. Strangely, fifteen minutes after Kyle called the numbers of the employees, he got a call from the NIA's datamatics centre, just informing him that new employees have been assigned as two employees had fallen sick. Now, this was strange. How did NIA know Kyle was trying to reach them? Now listen to this, Akram. Kyle generated keyboard logs of the new employees and he still has his team trying to understand. As soon as these two guys came in, there has been some activity on the logs. Databases have been accessed under guise of indexation searches. Kyle was in panic when he rushed to my place. He feels our phones are tapped as are our security apps are also run by the National Datamatics centre.

Akram felt blood draining from his face. He knew exactly what was going on. They had been compromised. NIA had got the empowerment to break into a RAW 'Dark' project.

"Akki, are you thinking what I'm thinking. Are we fucked?"

"Wait Sammy, let me think..."

"Get Kyle here... wait... don't call him on his phone. Call his Bengali girlfriend. You have her number?"

Samdup tried to jog his memory. He had done a background verification on her and had stored her number. What was her bloody name? Annie... Angie... Angela... yes Angela. He browsed his phone... and then used his other prepaid phone he had for security reasons. He called the number.

"Hello ji... hello."

"Hi, is that Angela?"

"Yes, but who are you asshole? Calling at 2 in the night!"

"Shut up, and give the phone to Kyle now!"

"What K... Kyle... he... hey don't grab my phone!"

Samdup had found him.

"Kyle here. Samdup sir, is this you?"

"Kyle... Samdup here. Your mother was born in Kolkata."

Samdup and Kyle had always had a code to identify the authenticity of the other and each of the five code phrases also had a direction for action. This particular phrase meant

Kyle was to reach Samdup at an alternate number using an alias phone.

"Give me twenty, boss." And Kyle hung up.

In five minutes, Akram Khan had already gone and slipped on a pair of jeans and a T-shirt. His mind was racing.

Samdup's phone rang

"Yeah Kylie baby... you okay?"

"Yes sir, what the hell is going on?"

"Here speak to Akram sir..."

"Akram sir... oh you are with him... holly golly!"

"Kyle, listen very carefully. In the last five days, has any of the new placements by NIA Datamatics centre asked for a mock hacking drill?"

"Mock hacking drill? I don't think so... I ususally get a notification as systems go into a downtime for two hours. Oh fuck. Hold on... yes. Four days back the new placement... some guy called Pradyuman insisted on a mock Kazakhistan sourced cyber attack. He said he wanted to be sure and that NIA had asked for some standard certification."

Akram heard this and his suspicions were confirmed. The phone fell from his hands and he groaned and leaned back into the chair in his living area.

Samdup grabbed the phone and told Kyle to stay by the phone.

"What's wrong, Akki? What the hell is wrong?" He was holding Akki by his shoulders. His younger brother was part of Project Chexo and had been inserted three years back.

"Sammy, you recall the crisis protocols we wrote?"

"Yes, of course."

"Tell me, what were the three steps when we saw the first signs of an attempt to break into our firewalls?"

Samdup stared at Akki. His thoughts rushed to the protocol document and he recalled the first three steps.

"Of course I recall:

- *Shut down networks from all external pipes*
- *Run safety programmes on the now alienated network to check for system security*
- *Back up Priority 1 and 2 files in local drives*

And lastly, if system was found infected, the physical drives were removed from local station and transported to back up site."

"Sammy, when we ran the cyber attack drill a month back, what was the need to do it again? Where are the Priority 1 and 2 files now? *Where are the bloody files with location and identity details of our insertions?"*

Sammy stared at Akki and now he got what was happening.

He dialled Kyle's personal number back.

"Kyle, trace this asshole Pradyuman. Pick him up and bring him to Holiday Home in Bengali Market."

"Noted. Will reach 03.15."

"Kyle, party needs some snacks. Get them please."

Kyle noted and was already shortlisting six of his best team mates in the RAW protection squads.

Akram was staring at Samdup. He had never thought he would need a personal phone. He grabbed Sammy's phone and called Swamy's phone. On the second ring, he disconnected the phone. Then he called the phone again, and disconnected the phone again on the second ring.

In eighteen seconds, the phone rang.

"Yes, Akram... it has to be you, right?

"Yes sir."

"So, tell me champ, who is giving you a hard time?"

In a minute Akram had narrated the status to Swamy. It took Swamy a few seconds to respond.

"Akram, always a good time to get back home, isn't it? Good night Akram. Call me tomorrow."

Akram received the message loud and clear. He had been given instructions to wrap up Project Chexo. Initiate extract and protect sequence for all the eighteen implants and warn them so they could warn the local assets.

"Let's go to the Holiday Home, Sammy."

CHAPTER 11
EXTRACTION

New Delhi
2015

RAW had seventy-six 'holiday homes' around the world. In India, whilst they did not run operations, yet six holiday homes had been set up. These were mostly near points of entry and exit, like airports and seaports. There was a holiday home administrator – Mr Banerjee in Delhi – who coordinated these homes. They were mostly used by operatives when they were in 'fight or flight' mode. Often, locally recruited resources needed to be protected or debriefed. Hence these homes were transformed to meet specific requirements. They had enough food supply for ten residents for a month at any given time. Each location had a caretaker nicknamed CT. CT appointments were a must for each RAW recruit. It was also sometimes meted out as a punishment. It was likely that a CT could be at a location for even a year without the facility being ever used. State of the art communication as well as a well stocked armoury were other facilities provided to 'guests'.

Samdup had used a holiday home only in Shanghai on his last tour two years back.

Akram had gone in to quickly inform Aarti that he may be out for a couple of days. He had a ready bag and he dumped in some extra jeans and t-shirts for Sammy. When he got back out into the living room, he could see Samdup in action on his phone. Akram knew the situation was incredible. They were now at war with their own government. They were not trained for this. Samdup had already coordinated their arrival at the Bengali Market holiday home. Akram gestured to Samdup and they tiptoed down to the driveway. Samdup signalled to Akram that there could be lookouts monitoring his house. Akram motioned Samdup to follow him and took him through the garage to the rear door into the rear alley. They quickly jogged parallel to the Hanuman Mandir lane. It was now 4 a.m. Spotting an autorickshaw, Samdup shook the driver up and Akram and Samdup were soon on their way to Bengali Market.

CT Bhishambar Nath was recruited by the RAW from college. He graduated from the School of Middle Eastern Languages of Punjab University. He was soon nicknamed Bhishu. Bhishu could speak five languages that were used in the middle east. After his initial two-year training, Bhishu had a terrible first project in Qatar. In what could be just bad luck, the local asset he tried to recruit in Doha, a gorgeous Qatari bar server in a hotel in Doha, turned out to be a Qatari secret service asset and blew Bhishu's cover. He was extracted with some damage, but fortunately, in one piece. He requested for a Delhi location so he could be with his ailing father for as much time as possible. The CT position was given to him three months back and he was almost into depression because of the monotony of the job. Today was about to be different. He had received a message from Mr Bannerjee to expect nine guests. He was given three leads and rest he wasn't told about. At 2.15 a.m. his phone buzzed and he saw a group of men in all black at the main door. He asked for the entry credentials from Kyle and let them in.

Kyle was accompanied by six of the RAW protection forces team. He nodded to Bhishu as he entered and Bhisu shook his hand introducing himself.

"Hi, I am CT106. Do you want any food?"

"Hi CT 106. Not now. Please go into Secure Mode immediately please. Only communicate to RAW entities, please."

"Oh sure. You're the boss. Bannerjee called to nominate you as lead guest so I am to do anything you demand. Give me a minute while I initiate the sequences for secure mode."

In secure mode, the CT had to ensure that all communication links and systems operated in encrypted state. In this mode, only the Chief Guest had authority to communicate with the outside world.

Kyle looked at his team and barked quick orders.

"Please take a look at the Holhome plan and take charge of the location please. We are in secure mode so you know what we need to do."

While the six scampered quickly to take help from the CT for the floor plans, Kyle took the access card from CT and accessed the communication centre. The Holhome communication centre was integrated with an Israeli satellite and did not use any Indian interface. Some smart RAW manager was paranoid about secrecy and used the operations funds to rent a bloody satellite. God bless him, thought Kyle. He had fired up the servers and he knew, that night was going to be fun. He tried to locate the data centre chap, but he knew he wouldn't find him. The address drew a blank and since yesterday, he had not shown up at work.

CT106 barked out from the reception. "Two unknown at entrance. Please advise action. Identify on monitor 6, please.

Kyle looked up at the monitor and identified Boss and Akki sir.

"Allow please."

CT106 allowed entry to the two gents. They had to go through three stage entrance frames. Each frame had a reinforced steel door.

Akki and Samdup reached the reception where Kyle was waiting for them.

He smiled at Akki sir and Boss.

"Looks like a busy night, Boss."

Akram looked at Kyle. It was just the attitude he loved. He knew it was in Tibetan teachings, this ability to stay calm in the middle of chaos.

"K, I guess you didn't find that Datamatics guy?"

"No, sir. All contacts were fake. Tried NSA, but no response at all."

"Okay, is the conference room secure?"

"Absolutely, sir. We are uplinked into the Abraham 22, our favourite satellite."

Akki walked swiftly into the conference room and with Kyle and Samdup in, was shutting the door, when CT106 stepped in just as the door was closing.

"Excuse me, what the hell do you think you are doing?" Samdup had already reached out to grab CT106's hand.

"Sir, I am to shadow Primary Guest at every stage sir. Sorry, you are an unknown and I will not leave the room with you two alone with my Primary Guest," he looked at Kyle.

Kyle stepped closer to CT106 and whispered into CT106 ear and in a flash, CT106 stepped back and rushed outside.

"What was all that about?" Samdup was amused and asked Kyle.

"Aha, nothing sir. You forget that I was a CT as well in Goa. I know how the poor guy feels. I just told him we are expecting company and he should get ready for level 1 defence in case of an attack on the Holhome. It will keep him busy!" Kyle smiled and closed the door.

Akram dropped into the chairs and leaned to stretch back and thought of his next moves.

"Okay, gentlemen, I have the go ahead from Swamy to wind down Project Chexo and start extraction sequence. Our own security apparatus has some conflict. Our databases have been compromised. NSA has all our back-up files. So, I don't know what they are doing with the list, but we have to immediately start our extraction protocols. Get them all out – all eighteen."

Samdup and Kyle stared in shock. All the years of hardwork would disappear in a matter of days. Samdup had mixed feelings. His brother was part of the insertions in China and it was almost one year since he had met him. The last few years of being part of the Indian government had been quite revealing. Of course, there were fine people in the team. Akram, for starters, was like a godfather to his son. It all boiled down to politics as Tibetans were seen as a bargaining chip for India and that would never change. Finally, he always said that a foreigner would always be a foreigner, even in the house of a hospitable host.

Bringing attention back to the conference room, he noticed Kyle had taken control of the central console to start work. Kyle had matured into quite an asset. For Samdup, he was like his second son. He had a unique blend of raw bravery and combat skills and knowledge of technology. Samdup went up to the chair between Akram and Kyle, and began giving Kyle instructions.

"Bring up on screen the last known locations of logins of assets, please."

Kyle hammered away at the keyboard.

The 60 inch LED screen in the room came alive and within seconds the screen turned into a geographic map of China. The screen flashed with green dots of last login locations of all eighteen assets.

Project Chexo worked on the classic guideline of 'Plant and Grow'. Inserts were left on their own for long periods of time for them to adapt and settle into a new environment. The espionage craft dictated that any asset must first build his neighbourhood cocoon. That means enough local resources who would certify that they knew him well and would vouch for his genuineness. So every asset worked in the first year or two to get to know all resources within 500 metres. For instance, at the local store, leaving a handsome tip always won you friends.

Of the eighteen, the youngest was inserted twelve months back. As Akram stared at the screen, he noticed three red flashes. He looked at Samdup. Samdup was staring at the screen. Tibet, Chengdu and Tianjin.

Samdup asked Kyle, "Bring up the last contact history of all three, please."

In seconds, the screen split into three segments and all emails, encrypted messages, and voice messages came up in chronological order for each of the three implants. The top of each vertical was a photograph of the asset and key essentials like date of insertion, current role, and specific project that they were working on.

Kyle read the summary for each.

"Okay, these three have not checked in on the last agreed fortnight check and neither have they escalated any information. It's nothing to worry though, as it's common sometimes for no contact. We would have ideally almost 10% 'red markers' here, but for a protocol change, we had passed on ten days back to just change the encryption logic in their communication procedures. Dema, Chinpa and Kalden had not logged in and our data centre had followed the process to establish a specific reach out. And after receiving a comfort flag had not escalated the matter. Of course, they should have green coded these three, but looks like they forgot."

Samdup nodded, "Okay, so then are we okay?"

Akram reacted, "Did you say data centre?"

Kyle responded, "Yes sir, when we are unable to get a time bound log, we send out an alarm sequence on all the contact devices. And if there is no response in two hours, we record it as an emergency. In this case, as the three must have responded, the data centre green flagged all of them."

Akram was staring at Samdup.

"Gentlemen, you are talking of our own data centre? Why the fuck do you think we are here today. No rules apply. We have to believe that our internal infrastructure is compromised. We just don't know who to trust. Please bring up the confirmation messages from all three please."

Kyle worked at the keyboard and the screen turned blank for a second before flashing:

Data not available.

Kyle tried once again, but there was no information.

"There is no information of the confirmations."

Samdup was in panic. He got up.

"This is ridiculous. What's going on, Akki? You think NIA is now engaging with our team in China and using them for some covert operation without telling us and asking our agents not to communicate with us?"

Akram looked at both Samdup and Kyle and related to them the debrief Swamy had given to him after his meeting in the PMO.

Samdup was in shock. "What are you saying, Akki? That the government, to win a trade deal, is happy to exchange information with China?"

"I don't know, Sammy. I really don't know. Okay, let's not waste time. We need our team back. Kyle, initiate our Quick Check Out procedure please."

The QCO process sent out an alarm message through all possible communication channels to the eighteen assets. Mobiles, watches, and laptop sets. All devices were geared to send out a message to the asset. Within minutes, each asset had to send back a confirmation that they were secure, uncompromised and ready for instructions. If an asset didn't respond in ten minutes, contact would be made with a local resource that the asset had developed and nominated by the implant to help in case of emergency. This resource was then contacted, and using some sob story, was asked to go and check on the asset. According to the engagement rules, no implant knew the other except for cases where mentoring was required. This was to ensure that even if one was captured, the others were not compromised.

Kyle had already typed out the sequence.

"QCO initiated, response awaited..."

The screen now turned back to the map of China and all eighteen locations turned red and were flashing waiting for confirmation.

Akram had meanwhile updated Swamy on using the secure network in the Holhome. Swamy heard him out and the only one message in response was, "Akki, just get them out. For god's sake, asap!"

Every single minute after the QCO initiation was pure torture. All three had eyes glued on the screen for the confirmations to pour in and the red flashing lights turning green. Twenty minutes had passed and all eighteen lights were still blinking red.

Akki walked up to the screen and turned to Kyle.

"Kyle, how many hours have passed since the screw up in the data centre?"

"Seventy-eight hours forty-three minutes, sir." Kyle knew what Akki sir was thinking. The worst possible scenario – the asset list being leaked to external parties.

Akram could sense a dark cloud looming over his head. This was his worst nightmare come true. My own government. Sneaking the list from his data centre. He could sense the rage build up within him. He could see a crestfallen Samdup staring at the screen. He could imagine the thoughts that would be racing through his head. Bloody Indian government, sacrificing the Tibetans for the sake of some deal with the Chinese.

Twenty-eight minutes had passed. Not one light flashed green.

Akram took a decision.

"Okay, Kyle who is our best local asset for our asset who aced the academy? Chinpa... where and who?"

Kyle typed out commands and the screen had data being thrown up.

"Chinpa...local alias Yu Yan. Implant location Tibet. She has not been able to develop a local asset, but has given an emergency contact of the fruit seller opposite her flat. She has recorded that he fancied her and always looked out for her."

"Call him. Is your local dialect good?" Akram asked Kyle.

"Err. Not at all, sir. But we have resources here who are geared to do this, sir. I can get that done on a merged call right now."

With this, Kyle looked at Samdup who merely nodded at Kyle.

Kyle dialled an India number from the screen and a young girl picked the phone.

Kyle spoke to her quickly and after warning her, merged the call to an outbound call to the fruit seller.

Akram could clearly hear the conversation and he could see Samdup and Kyle's facial reactions. They were looking at each other and he could make out that something was not right.

In twenty-five seconds, the conversation ended.

Kyle looked at Akram.

"Sir, yesterday morning he said that he was loading fruit onto his cart when a luxury car that could have only belonged to some senior government machinery had screeched to a halt in front of him. He saw three men and a woman help Yu Yan get into the car and they sped away. He said that he could see Yu Yan was not feeling well as they had to almost carry her into the car. He presumed her friends had come to help her. They were there for only a minute or so."

Samdup's eyes were now taking on a sharp determined look.

"Akki, we are in trouble. The team is compromised. Action started in China twenty-four hours back. They probably had the list in three hours after it was extracted from our centre."

Akram could only stare at Samdup as the weight of this news crushed his mind with pictures of the eighteen that flashed in his mind. The eighteen men and women. *Ya Allah, reham*! He stood up and rage swept through his body. He raised his fists and pounded the table. Samdup rushed to Akram and held him back.

Rage turned to panic.

"No Sammy! No! No! This cant be happening!"

Without realising it, Samdup had just given Akram a tight slap on his cheek. The sound of the slap effected a complete silence in the room.

"You're a trained RAW operative, damnit. Is this the way to lose control? My own brother is there, Akki. Get a hold of yourself. We need to figure out what to do."

Samdup shook Akki by his shoulders.

Akram grabbed a bottle of water from the table and gulped it down.

He looked at Samdup and Kyle.

"Am fine, am fine. It's okay. Thanks!"

"Our ten-minute protocol got over some time back. Yu Yan is certainly in government custody and while I hate to admit it, I must share that I'm almost certain that the Chinese government has all our eighteen in custody somewhere. Of course, I am certain that they are alive as they will take them at least two weeks to debrief them."

Akram got up and walked across to the main door, gesturing to Kyle to open the access door.

As soon as Akram walked outside with his bloodshot eyes and unkempt hair, he got a glare from the Holhome CT.

Akram stared back.

"Where's the loo?"

CT106 marked a door on the opposite side of the reception and Akram swiftly walked across to the marked door.

Cold water can be a blessing to calm one's nerves. As Akram let his hands into the basin full of water, he bent and put his head under the water for a good twenty seconds. He stared at the face that looked back at him. Fucked by my own government! My eighteen operatives in Chinese custody going through severe torture. Sammy's brother... no trace. Yu Yan, the find of the century... no trace. Indians betrayed by Indians!

Akram stared at his face. He had caused the loss of eighteen operatives in two days. Without realising it, his mind released a dump of adrenal in his body and his hand balled into a fist and slammed the mirror in front of him.

"*Noooooooooooo!*" A scream escaped his lips just as CT106 burst into the washroom and grabbed Akram from behind.

"What the hell...." He could hardly hold back Akram whose bleeding hands continued to hit the broken mirror. The protection detail team also arrived on the scene. Three of them grabbed and dragged a screaming Akram back to the conference room. A shocked Kyle had already grabbed a first-aid box.

It took some time for three of them to extract the last glass particle from Akram's hands and bandage them.

Akram sat in stoic silence, his expression unwavering from the eighteen red blinking spots on the map of China. He grabbed Samdup and hugging him he whispered,

"Sammy, I don't know what I'll do, but I can tell you that I will die trying to get my team back. Do you believe me?"

Samdup hugged him back.

"Akki, we know you will give up your life for these youngsters. No one could have asked for a better mentor or a better run operation. It's not your fault. But I need your brains, Akram Khan. Let's do it for these poor souls."

CHAPTER 12
MUTINY

New Delhi
2015

It was 5 a.m. Akram had updated Swamy Sir and was now sitting in the lawns of Swamy's home along, with his two dogs, who were busy grabbing biscuits from Akram's hands.

Akram could only watch as Swamy leaned back in his garden chair, tea cup in hand and staring at the light from the rising sun as it slowly filled the horizon with golden warmth.

Akram had filled in Swamy with details and Swamy could very clearly put two and two together. Swamy too had briefed Akram on his meetings with the CDC as well as the action taken on Freddy Daruwala. Of course, Akram knew exactly what had happened, but this op was much too complex with his own country's chief having engineered it. He wasn't trained for this.

"What happened to your hand?" Swamy asked without even looking down at Akram's hands.

"Oh, nothing much sir, just tripped over my side table."

Swamy looked down at him and murmured, "*Holhome ke mirror ki cost kaun dega*?"

Akram looked down and kept quiet.

Swamy had thought his moves through and got up from his chair.

"Come, walk with me."

Akram followed him as he strolled across the lawns.

"So, Akram, we have a mole. No one could have breached the data centre in this smart way without knowing how it operates and how data gets backed up, etc. I have given this much thought. I don't know... right or wrong... but we have to choose sides now. To save our eighteen, we may have to take actions that may brand you as a traitor. Hope it's clear that it's you who has to now take charge. You will have the operating funds at your disposal. In minutes, your UAE account will get a credit of USD 4 mn. That's almost 32 crore rupees. These funds are not accounted, so it doesn't worry me. The banker will call you and the codes are the usual ones."

Swamy paused as he saw a squirrel race up the tree to escape the dogs who were running toward the tree.

"The one and the only one person who can be the mole is Freddy Daruwala. I had his security detail infiltrated a week back and he has met the CDC on at least three occasions after meeting me, even though he was instructed *not* to contact the CDC. He is the only link you have, Akram. You know what you have to do. Compromise his loyalty and turn him and use him. Do not, I repeat, do not use any vanishing theme as the CDC will be alerted. I expect that they will imagine that as Freddy thinks the check-in is twelve days away, they have time before you discover the missing eighteen. As this will be my last conversation with you till you can emerge out in the open, I can only share with you that there is some linkage to a senior political entity in China – Liu Rongji. Liu is the deputy chairperson of the Politburo Standing Committee. This entity and CDC have been engaging in several discussions over the last two months. Don't ask me how I know this. I also know that the PMO has organised a reception dinner for this asset next week on Thursday. The venue is shocking. It's the Rashtrapati Bhawan. But there is no official announcement and everything is being kept under wraps."

Akram was awestruck at the information Swamy sir had access to.

"Sir, you have an asset in the Rashtrapati Bhawan?"

Swamy looked at Akram, "Akram, this is as high as it can go, so be careful of what you do."

In a rather uncharacteristic gesture, Swamy leaned forward and patted Akram on his cheeks and then held him by his shoulder.

"I am sorry, Akram. As your leader, I could not see this coming. I have failed you. And these eighteen are my responsibility."

Akram's eyes welled up and he stepped closer to Swamy and gave him a hug.

"Akram, get them back. Just get them back."

With this, Swamy turned around and walked purposefully to his house, leaving Akram at the main gate."

Akram was now carrying the alternate device Kyle had hooked up for him. He dialled Samdup.

"Am on the way. Ask Kyle to access personnel records in the RAW mainframe. Tell him he can use Swamy's usual anagram as login. and I am sending him the passkey on his instrument. Get access to Freddy Daruwala's file and pick up any of his regular house staff. Bring him to the Holhome."

At 7 a.m., Akram had joined the team in the Bengali Market Holhome. Kyle had already retrieved Freddy's file. Given the nature of the work, all personnel files were very detailed. They were eighty pages thick and had everything anyone could know about any individual. RAW also undertook three surveillance initiatives every year for senior staff members. As chances of corruption and espionage were common, this was regular practice.

Kyle had already studied key parts of the file. Akram filled in both of them. Whilst Kyle was not security cleared for most of this level of information, Akram knew that it was war and that too a sensitive one. And a soldier needed to know why he was fighting.

Kyle looked at the file and pointed out to the last recorded daily routine for Freddy.

"So, Babaji goes to Lodi gardens with his dog at 8 a.m. and then spends an hour there. I also checked that his security detail has three guys and my protection team leader knows his security detail chap.

Akram responded, "So, then we don't need to grab his house staff. Re-direct to Lodi and pick him up without drawing attention please. Sammy, you go with them and make it look like Swamy has asked for an urgent meeting. He must still be at Lodi... go grab him."

It was a long wait for Akram and almost an hour elapsed when the CT announced the team had returned. Akram stood at the reception door to watch three burly men and Samdup escort a shocked Freddy into the Holhome. A pity, but it looked like Mr Daruwala had had a bit of a fall. His forehead had a cut and blood trickling down to his white t-shirt.

Samdup smiled at Akram. "Our guest has arrived. His security detail was convinced to go home with the dumb dog, so we have a good two hours. Sorry, Freddy hit his forehead by accident on the car door."

Akram glared at Freddy while Freddy was turning crimson in anger.

"Akram, what the hell is this! How dare you guys fool me into coming here?"

Freddy turned around in a sudden action grabbing Samdup's right hand. Turning him around, he tried to push him down. In a second, Samdup had his free left hand on Freddy's forearm and he pressed one of the 108 pain points the human body has. The pressure was so intense that Freedie screamed and dropped to the floor. Samdup wasn't finished. Before Akram could stop him, he had given Freddy three quick punches. One to his throat and the other just in the middle of his chest. Freddy didn't know what hit him. He could hardly breathe and was now gasping,holding his chest.

Akram rushed to grab Freddy.

"Sammy, are you crazy? We need him to talk."

Akram and the protection team helped Freddy onto his feet and dragged him into the conference room. Kyle was already massaging Freddy's throat and chest, trying to get the blood flowing again. A wet cloth was palced on Freddy face.

It took almost twenty minutes for Freddy to gain normalcy. Samdup knew that if he wanted, he could have simply killed him with two pressure points. He was worried that he almost had. Akram was right, we needed him.

Akram sat next to Freddy.

"Sir, are you okay? Freddy, can you hear me... Freddy?"

Freddy looked back at Akram and grabbed a bottle of water from the table. As he unscrewed the cap, he glared at Samdup.

"You fucking chinky! How dare you assault me? I want my phone, damnit. And you Akram, you and this team will spend years in jail if I don't have you executed myself!"

Akram pointed his finger at the large screen that still had the map with eighteen red blinking dots.

"Freddy, do you know what these are?"

Freddy sat up and stared at the screen.

"You guys are using the Israeli Sat El Ava and tracking China. I know all this, Akram. What are you teaching me, huh? I helped buy the damn machinery!"

"Freddy, look at the eighteen blinking red dots."

"Okay, must be eighteen... so what are they? Most famous brothels for you?"

A loud slap resounded in the room. Freddy was in shock as Akram had just hit him across his face.

"Freddy, listen to me, you traitor. These are the eighteen assets of Project Chexo that we told you about in China. They are all missing and haven't checked in. If you don't help me find each one of them, Freddy, Allah kasam, I will cut your body into eighteen pieces!"

Akram saw Freddy's expressions soften. He stumbled up from his chair and stared at the screen.

"Our assets haven't reported in? What about emergency contact protocol? Have we tried that? When were they to check in? Have we run QCO?"

He looked around the room, "Answer me, goddamn it!"

Akram looked at Kyle and gave a quick nod.

Kyle updated Freddy. Freddy was an old hand, of course, and knew all the protocols of implants. Akram closely watched him. He had a good instinct for this. He knew Freddy was not lying.

Freddy looked at Akram, "Why did you initiate QCO? Did you suspect something? How did you know something was wrong?"

Akram stared at Freddy and shared everything with Freddy. He new he didn't have to courage to beat information out of a senior colleague, so he had to take his chances now.

Freddy crashed into the chair. "Holy fuck! The data centre. So that's what CDC wanted!"

Akram sat next to Freddy.

"Freddy, I don't think you meant to get 18 RAW agents into trouble, did you? Sir, you are my senior. For god's sake, please level with us. You can see we are close to waging a full covert operation on our own government and I will do it even if I am hanged for this. I will go to any length, sir, and if that means I have put your head under water or beat the damn information out of you, I will."

"Yes, Akram, I deserve it. Please kill me."

Freddy was looking down to the floor and Akram knew he had done the right thing by trusting Freddy.

"As you do know I have been working with the PMO and the CDC for over eight months now on a project to neutralise the China threat. Our Economic Advisor sent a paper to PMO last year, waxing eloquently about how the centre of economic power was moving from West to East, from USA to China.

Given the influence that China has on our neighbours, we know that China has managed to infiltrate the thought process in Pakistan, Nepal, Bangladesh, Myanmar and even Sri Lanka to a pro-China view. You note all the trouble we are having with our neighbours. In that document, a mathematical model was generated that showed how, if we ally with China, we can increase our trade volumes to a surplus, neutralise our neighbours, reduce our defense costs in Siachin and along the northeast. It was forecasted that in five years, India can gain a value of 50-100 Bn USD."

Freddy was now walking up and down in front of the large screen with a bottle of water in hand.

"The PMO charged CDC to work on this. Given my history with the CDC, as we had worked on three covert ops in the last fifteen years, the CDC advised PMO that we should take some informal advice from RAW as well. As the matter was extremely sensitive and with the entire politics with elections next year, the usual protocols of informing key intelligence personnel were ignored. What's more, I was told that there is a leak in RAW. In fact, the CDC alluded that Swamy was under investigation."

Akram felt the earth move. Was his head spinning? Swamy sir, no way!

"Hold on Akram, before you jump to any new thoughts. I had done my own elaborate investigation and I can now tell you it was all bullshit. It was just a lollipop thrown at me that after Swamy, it had to be me. I got suckered into this and started cooperating with the CDC. We now needed something to trade with China. Among other trade ideas, one idea thrown by the Chinese was ‘total and complete transparency’. They said if we were to start as friends, we must demonstrate that we were truly friends, and for that, both the countries had to extract their implants but with information to the counter party six hours after extraction, so they could ensure they had neutralised all local networks. So, one of the ‘non negotiable’ conditions was that we disclose all our assets, details six hours after extraction.

“The CDC and PMO assured me that RAW may refuse to disclose the list, but we must see the list as we suspected ‘Swamy was a traitor’ and hence I guided the CDC to take help from the NIA datamatics centre to get to the list. And your attitude didn’t help at all. I suspected that you were close to Swamy and didn’t know what was going on.

“But the list was to be extracted next week, two days before the visit of the main guy who is negotiating for the Chinese.”

Akram remarked, “Liu Rongji”.

Now it was Freddy’s turn to be surprised.

“How the hell do you know this?”

“Go on, Freddy.”

Freddy was in shock. He was almost wanting to earn Akram’s trust and he knew there was no place for lies.

“Well, we were to study the list so we could share some broad titillating bits where all are implants worked to make the Chinese salivate and then pull you in to extract them and then release the list to the Chinese. What you are now telling me is that the plan to take the list was activated three days back, a week ahead of schedule, and now all eighteen of our agents are incommunicado? So, we are now of the view that the fucking idiot of someone in PMO has already shared the list with the Chinese and they are in custody, right?"

"Right. Custody or some may have put up a fight and may be dead, for all we know."

Freddy looked down at the table.

"Akram, let's grab the son of a bitch CDC. Bring the asshole here and give me an hour with him. Akram, I know we don't share a good relationship. For god's sake, I was an agent in the field. I would never never put my team in danger, Akram. Believe me, please. Our own government can't do this... please... believe me, Akram!"

Akram was certain that Freddy was now telling the truth. Espionage was all a mind game. Freddy had tried to be smart, but got outsmarted. Happens all the time. Of course, in this case it was happening in your own house. Akram contemplated his next move. His ultimate goal was to get his team back. Freddy was right. They could consider kidnapping the CDC. The very thought was shocking – a senior RAW officer planning to kidnap the CDC. Many decades ago, the British government in India had branded his great grandfather as a traitor. Was he destined to earn a similar tag? He turned back to Freddy.

"Freddy, how would you like to earn your honour back, you useless fucking pig?"

CHAPTER 13
AUTOPHAGY

New Delhi
2015

"What the hell is Autophagy? What the hell are you talking about?" Freddy was looking at Akram. He was now at a stage where he could go to any length to get the eighteen back.

"Freddy, it's now well researched that the best way to heal your body is to get your own cells to clean up all the unwanted cells in the body. Your body's cells will turn inwards to find sources of food and they will naturally pick stuff that is useless to the body like extra fat cells, cancer growth cells etc, etc. We are now faced with that, Freddy. Rather, you are faced with it, because let's face it, you're the dumb RAW officer who may have managed to get eighteen operatives in China captured. Some may even be dead."

Freddy was crestfallen. He knew Akram was right.

"Okay Akram. I accept that. I am with you. What do you want to do?"

"We will have to cleanse our nation of some unwanted cells. Who is the mastermind of this trade deal?"

"You mean MEA (Ministry of External Affairs). They are only the execution arm. It's not the MEA."

Akram looked at the team in the conference room with the eighteen red lights blinking.

"No, Freddy, it's not the MEA. Who wants this deal done and why? Who benefits most from this deal?"

"Well, that would be the NDP – National Democratic Party, right? Oh, I see what you are saying... Are you mad?"

"No, Freddy, it's true. The leader of the NDP is Shri Narottam Singh, our Prime Minister. He is the kingpin. He has to put this as a condition to the deal. The safe return of our eighteen agents. We have to cleanse this country now, Freddy."

"Are you mad, Akram? You will kidnap the Prime Minister of India?"

"Okay, gentlemen. This discussion stops here. Sammy, Kyle and Freddy, you are the only ones who have heard this. This will not leave this room. Freddy, this Chinese guy is coming to India. Please let me have it all. Do not leave out anything."

Freddy shrugged his shoulders and throwing his hands up in the air, started vomiting facts as only a trained espionage asset can do.

"The CDC is in charge of this visit. Seems the PMO wanted to shock and awe him and persuaded the President to extend a special invite. Unfortunately, it is not an official visit or the media would have got a whiff of it."

Freddy paused and recalled some pieces of conversation he overheard the CDC having.

"I can't be sure, but there is some damn connection to his children or child. The CDC was quite keen to clarify to someone that the child is fine or the children will be there. He comes in on the 23rd of September and the dinner is planned for that night. The Rashtrapati Bhawan (RB) staff have not been told yet. The PM, CDC, the Chinese and the President will attend. I think to ensure secrecy, the guest comes straight from airport and leaves RB at 11 p.m. for the airport. I guess they will want to close all the details. Elections aren't too far away, huh?"

Akram motioned Samdup to keep quiet.

"Freddy, can we instead kidnap this Chinese guy?"

"Akram, how? Where? It's good idea. He is a senior guy, but he lands and gets Z+ security cover. Is at RB for two hours before returning to the airport. Will you hit the motorcade? Kill our own security detail guys?"

Akram thought of the scenario. Freddy was right. It was impossible. And there's no way that he would kill any of his own countrymen.

"Freddy, call up the CDC. He doesn't know we have figured this. You told him our bi-weekly check is next week, right? So he still doesn't think we know. Go meet him. Do some field work for a change. This is really your chance to help, Freddy. I don't want to use harsh words and I am sorry we had to get a little violent. I do believe you have been played by the CDC. Time to play back, Freddy. Help me! Help your team!"

Freddy was staring at Akram. How wrong he was about this man. He realised that pure jealousy had been the reason for his mistrust.

"Akram..." He moved forward and held Akram by his shoulders.

"I was so wrong about you. I am proud of what you've set up. I was just jealous that I could not ever dream of setting up Project Chexo. Listen, even now Project Chexo is the PMO's trump card to get a fantastic deal for this country. I promise you, I won't let eighteen indians die for this. I am grateful you guys didn't just slit my throat the moment I walked in."

Freddy got up. "Kyle, get me one of your com gadgets. I will communicate using that. I will check back every twenty-five minutes with a message into the sever. Kyle will put up escalation messages in case of failure. If I do fail, you guys do what you see fit."

Akram nodded at Kyle, who grabbed the main door and shouted to the CT, "CT, officer transport please, asap!" Kyle grabbed an encrypted enabled phone and handed it to Freddy.

Freddy nodded and walked out of the conference room.

As soon as the door had shut, Akram looked at Kyle with a quizzical look.

Kyle nodded and gave a thumbs up sign. The special encryption enabled phone sets that were being used had a special application that allowed an admin to track and remotely use the applications on the phone. Freddy was given the set which had this remote activation application. Kyle could now activate the cameras or listen to any conversation on the phone.

Akram did think Freddy would help, but he had to be sure.

"I think I am taking a bet on Freddy. But can never be sure, right?"

Kyle looked at Akram and remarked.

"Boss, I want to request that we get Norbu into the picture. He's heading the protection detail today that was assigned to me. He was outstanding in the Myanmar Training Centre's (MTC) simulations."

The RAW training centre in Myanmar spread over 100 acres had 20-25 life-like simulation environments.

"From hot pursuits to extractions. If you recall the armed forces operations in Myanmar, Norbu was the detailing specialist."

The Detailing Specialist was the chief architect for any operation. He evaluated the situation and then designed the most suitable plan for the said situation. Akram looked at Samdup for his opinion and Sammy gave his usual right eyebrow twitch that expressed his approval.

"Okay, Kyle, you know the situation. Go out and take him to the four-seater discussion room and let him work on this. Our target is to get to our Chinese friend and use him as a ransom with our PM to negotiate the release of our eighteen agents."

Even as he spoke, Akram could not but think of how this would end for him and his RAW team. Anyway, he could not think of that. Right now, the Project Chexo senior team had one and only one agenda. Extraction.

"Kyle, get in two data seekers to assist you asap. You can't do this alone. Freddy's phone needs a full-time resource. Sammy, I need you to plan the extraction. Plan three exits. We have to assume everyone cannot be at one place. The regional level command centres will have the first right to interrogate the team. You recall the junkie you recruited years back? Use him. I have your Dubai funds routing company's details. I am transferring two mn USD right now. I want these funds used up in three hours. No cap on expenses. No need for approvals. You are empowered to use the funds. Set up three routes."

Kyle nodded and got to work. Samdup too nodded and started accessing his contacts.

"I am going out and will be back in an hour. We will regroup in ninety minutes."

Akram walked out of the conference room. He found the CT on the reception desk, playing with a ball pen.

As soon as he saw Akram, he jumped up.

"Sir!"

"CT?" Akram stared at him.

Bhishu stared at him. Akram may have forgotten but Bhishu could not forget that Akram had been part of his Myanmar training schedule.

"CT 106... Sir, I was in Qatar, sir... and—"

Akram motioned with his hand asking him to stop talking.

"Bhishu, I don't forget guys who catch my attention. You aced the interrogation section in MTC. You speak four Middle eastern languages, but can only abuse in Punjabi."

He smiled at Bhishu and patted him on the shoulder.

Bhishu was taken aback. Akram sir remembered him.

"Sir, you are spot on. Anything I can do, sir?"

"Bhishu, the most important thing you can do is to keep the food coming to the team. You have to remind us to eat, right?" Akram smiled and motioned CT 106 to open the exits.

"Of course, Sir. Will do, sir."

Akram walked out and messaged Swamy, arranging for a meeting at Janpath. Some of the back lanes in Janpath, a large commercial hub in Delhi, were fantastic for discreet meetings. Plenty of crowds and several roadside corners to sneak into and have a chat.

Taking a three-wheeler to Janpath, Akram soon reached the corner where Swamy and he often met to have a quick chat. Just close by was a famous chhole kulche eatery. He decided to order a couple of plates while he waited. It was afternoon time and he could feel the lack of energy.

As he dug into the food, he felt someone slide right next to him wearing a baseball cap and dark glasses. Swamy smiled at Akram and picked one of his kulchas.

"Aah, this is certainly comfort food, eh? See what you north Indians have done to a simple Tam Brahm... huh!" Akram knew this was Swamy's favourite roadside food and he smiled at him.

"PMO thinks you've been compromised!"

Swamy almost choked on his kulcha. Grabbing the bottle of water and washing down the food, he blurted,

"What did you just say?"

Akram stared with all seriousness at Swamy.

"Not joking. The CDC has planted this thought that the RAW Chief is compromised. So they decided to keep you out of the mega deal. I had Freddy picked up. His interrogation has revealed this. I believe him."

Swamy was absorbing this incredible piece of information. He was now tracing back to his entire interaction with CDC. What could the CDC gain?

"Wow, then why haven't they taken action?"

"Well, not sure, but looks like the CDC may have used this to keep the control with himself. Anyway, we will deal with this later." With this, Akram quickly updated Swamy on the developments.

"Akram, this is pure treason, my boy. You are using RAW resources to mount an attack on the PM and his esteemed Chinese guests. You do know that if someone even gets a whiff of this, you will be shot and so will all the RAW resources in the Holhome. Akram, I think we should use a direct approach. Why don't we go straight to the PM? Appraise him and take his help."

Akram was taken aback at this suggestion.

"Sir, what are you saying? Will the PM trust you or me when CDC has already planted something in the PMO. I won't be surprised that as we speak somebody is planning a formal investigation of you. Of course, guess what Freddy already did. His desk research and gave you a clean chit..." Akram smiled as he said this. He saw Swamy smile back.

"So Freddy is a good boy now, eh?"

"I do think he got played by the CDC. He wants revenge. I have sent him on an info-farming trip to CDC. Let's see what he gets. No direct approach will work, sir. At best, if the Chinese feel India is having a rethink, they will simply do the vanishing trick with them and inform India that they never found anyone."

Swamy pondered over this. This was indeed how China may react. Akki was right.

"Akki, how will we even manage to do this? We are talking of the PM and a senior Chinese official."

Akram looked at Swamy.

"Sir, I am Project Lead for Chexo. These guys are on my beat. Let us please agree that our meeting never happened. I wanted to come and tell you that I will not give you any more updates now. I don't know how this will end." Akram got off the broken bench.

"I will always be proud of working with you, sir." As both

got up, Akram gave Swamy a bear hug before swiftly walking away into the crowds. Swamy watched one of his proteges embark on a suicidal plan. As they hugged, Swamy whispered, “Left front, walk away.”

After Akram had walked away to reach the main road, he got into a rickshaw. When they were some distance away, Akram took out a piece of paper folded into a small capsule put into his pocket by Swami when they had hugged. Akram opened it and saw a list of accounts and login ids with passwords and balances of the accounts. He noticed the total balance was USD 40 mn. He quickly took a picture with his phone. The last row had a contact number and a name – ‘Executive Search Vice President Akbar Ansari’.

Akram Khan had just been given access to almost 75 mn USD and the contact of the person who would be able to put together a team for Akram to use in a covert operation. *Ya Allah*, Akram thought, Swamy sir is planning for war! This would perhaps be the first time when a RAW unit may have to execute a plan in their home country. Unthinkable and yet Akram knew that they had no other choice. Any leak of the information that Akram or his team knew about may lead to a quick execution of all eighteen.

CHAPTER 14
DIDIMA

New Delhi
2015

Back at the Holhome, Akram noticed that Norbu was in an animated discussion with Kyle. Sammy was busy setting up the exit routes. Akram nodded to Kyle and he came into the conference room. The eighteen blinking red lights were a constant reminder to the team of their missing mates. Some may already be dead.

"Okay folks, we are cleared by the HQ to initiate this project. Kyle, get Norbu into this core team now. He might as well be in the loop."

Kyle ran out and soon came back with Norbu. Norbu was of average Tibetan height of 5 feet 5 inches. He had a taut square face and you could make out that he was in exceedingly good shape. Norbu stepped in and saluted smartly, "Sir!"

Akram nodded and asked Norbu to sit down.

"Norbu, Kyle seems have taken to you, eh? I hope you will bring in value. You know the situation we are in. So, you will join this group team as Chief Architect for this plan? Clear?"

"Clear, sir," Norbu responded. He was shocked that eighteen RAW agents were now in Chinese custody. This was a disaster.

"Okay boys, so let's start with Freddy baby. Where is that idiot?"

Kyle responded, “Sir, Freddy sir had two meetings since morning. He is really doing a damn good job. He is begging CDC to also invite him to meet the Chinese guy. He also had a usual meeting in RAW HQ with team members. He made some smart comments like, ‘I can’t get through Akram’ etc, etc. The CDC has promised to have a word with PMO to see if he can be invited.”

“Sammy, what do you have?”

“Okay, so we have now seeded funds to three extraction firms in China. They are essentially darkweb associates for smuggling Chinese in and out of countries. Work is on and in another four hours, I will have details of the plans.”

Akram nodded. Sammy had done a smart thing by using darkweb associates. Even if they were caught, funds could not be traced to RAW, so the Chinese would not guess what was being planned. He was sure Sammy had used the ‘reverse logic principle’ when setting up such extractions. How it worked was that entities in the target country were asked to help import illegal aliens into the country when they were actually planning to export folks out. Using this logic, the organiser could check the routes, but all he had to do was give a reverse instruction to the extraction company a few hours before the plan was executed. Dark web associates had received photographs and other details of all eighteen agents and alternate identities were being set up. A pity they could not use RAW’s ‘documentation centre’ which was really very good at this.

“So Norbu, what do you have for us? How do we get to this guy?”

Norbu looked at the team and nodded at Kyle.

Kyle punched commands into the keyboard and the screen dissolved to take shape into a map. Akram could make out details of New Delhi and soon he could make out the Indira Gandhi Airport.

Norbu took a laser pointer and began his briefing.

"Our target is landing at Delhi airport and will be escorted straight to the Rashtrapati Bhawan (RB)."

As he spoke, Akram saw that in a few hours he had made what is called a 'Opportunity Threat Index' .Using probability theory any extraction / assassination / kidnapping plotted at least three specific points where action may be initiated to achieve the primary objective of the plan. On a scale of 0 to 1, the index demonstrated the Chief Architect's view of the chances of success of each action point. What Akram was seeing was a bloody good index simulation.

"We have identified our three action points of A, B and C. A is in the airport itself, where we can grab him as he enters the airport after deplaning. Given CISF security, and now that he is being hosted at the RB, we can safely assume that at least a perimeter will be set up by the PBG as well. PBG was the 'President's Body Guards', the most prestigious armed forces regiment. They are in charge of protecting the President of India. We expect collateral civilian damage at twenty-five and armed detail casualty at fifteen. This sequence has a 0.25 index of success. The next action point is B, which is as the motorcade leaves the airport; action is executed at this specific route about near Aerocity just as they are about to get onto the highway. Index score of .3 and minimal civilian death, but armed combatant casualty may be as high as 30."

Akram was watching him with a sombre face. Any index count below .85 was usually a no go in RAW. Norbu went on.

"Our last extraction is the RB itself. Here the index is 0.11 and combatant casualty is at least eighteen."

Akram stared at Norbu with a sullen face.

"Mr Ace Chief Architect, weren't you told that I will not kill my own defense forces in this action? *Did you not hear what was bloody told*? What is this useless simulation you guys have done. It's a piece of shit!"

In sheer anger, Akram picked the bottle of water and threw it on the wall. "It's a bloody piece of shit. Kyle, what kind of an incompetent Tibetan you've placed before me? You useless noodle-sucking dimwit. You think I am going to kill members of the PBG. Are you stupid?"

Norbu, stung by the vicious attack, looked down at his feet.

Samdup got up and asked Norbu to leave. "Get out!"

As soon as Norbu left, Samdup raised his hands in exasperation at Akram.

"Akram, Norbu is a soldier. He just presented what he is good at. For him, it was just applying what you taught him, Akram. And by the way, it's terrible manners to be sucking noodles!"

Akram looked at Samdup and held his shoulder breaking into a smile.

"You bet it is, Sammy. Don't you understand, Sammy? I can't kill Indians. I can't... hey, just call Norbu."

Kyle got up and opened the door and Norbu walked back in.

"Norbu, I apologise. Please understand we cannot murder our own countrymen. I need this Chinese fellow without harming my own countrymen. Do you understand?"

"Understood, sir. I have checked and rechecked sir. It is not possible to execute or design any such plan, sir."

Akram leaned back on his chair recalling what Norbu had just shared.

"Guys, no way can we breach RB. We have to think of something. Have you seen those damn PBG recruits? Each guy is 6 feet 3 inches, built like a tank, carrying some of the most modern resources."

Norbu also added his views.

"Yes, Sir. Impressive regiment. I read they were called GGBG (Governor General's body guards) in1947, when India became independent. In fact, a fun fact is that GGBG was an acronym that was also interpreted as 'God's gift to Beautiful Girls'!

The group broke out in laughter. So did Akram. Norbu went on

"In fact sir, the Viceroy Of British India made them into a bit of a cult regiment. Entrance tests were bloody tough and the pay was much higher to prevent chances of corruption."

Akram responded to Norbu's information.

"Indeed. I recall this... the Viceroy must have used them in Kolkata!"

"No sir!" Norbu was all excited at the chance to show off his knowledge of Indian history. In fact, they were moved to Delhi somewhere in 1925 or 1918 to the Viceroy House."

Akram thought Norbu was like a kid refusing to give up his argument.

"No, dear boy, the Viceroy House was always in Kolkata. In fact, I recall someone in my family's history designed the Viceroy House in Kolkata."

Norbu was getting nervous at this battle of wits. Should he just give up? But he was dead sure he was right.

"Sir, I am truly sorry to sound stubborn, but the Viceroy House was to move to Delhi when the British capital moved to Delhi from Kolkata."

"Really, Norbu!" Akram sneered with sarcasm. "And where do you think is the Viceroy House in Delhi today – Chandni Chowk, eh?"

Norbu was puzzled. This was class five general knowledge.

"Sir, my apologies again. The Viceroy House was renamed Rashtrapati Bhawan."

Akram Khan absorbed this piece of information and thought that he must be looking like an uneducated nitwit. How could he not know this? As he grew up, his grandmother regaled him with stories of his family heritage in Kolkata. He knew that from his mother's side two generations back, they were Hindu Bengalis. His grandmother lived in Kolkata at their ancestral home and it had been almost a year since he had met her. Every Kolkata trip was full of mystery, intrigue as after dinner he would pester Didima to tell another story of India's freedom struggle and how his great-grandfather was a fantastic revolutionary. She would sometimes even show him photographs and small memorabilia.

He focused on his memory and he was dead sure that his great-grandfather had worked in the Viceroy House in Kolkata and was a known revolutionary. He even went to jail.

The very use of the words 'Viceroy House' had triggered a burst of memories for Akram. If the Viceroy House was Rashtrapati Bhawan, then had his great-grandfather worked in Delhi? How could that be? Why would the family stay in Kolkatta.

"Oh!" he reacted to Norbu and was still in deep thought.

He just could not but get this niggling thought that he was missing something to do with the Viceroy House and his great-grandfather. If he recalled correctly, the police arrested his great-grandfather for throwing explosives somewhere in Kolkata in the Viceroy House... no... or was it in Delhi? He recalled Didima's voice like a small child, mentioning to him about how the best plan for independence was cooked up in a coffee shop in Kolkata and how his great-grandfather was the key to the plan. Eventually he would sleep, but his mind still raced with the faded pictures his Didima kept with her. Her treasure box – a small bag yellow with age was full of trinkets, jewellery, and the small photo album. The very thought of his Didima and the beautiful ancestral house with the fifteen feet high ceilings took him to a very happy part of his life.

He felt a hand on his shoulder and he came to the present with a start. Samdup was gently shaking his shoulder.

"We haven't slept in some time. I suggest we all catch a power nap."

Akram shook his head.

"Team, we need a solution. Come on, Norbu, aren't you the guy who used a fly drone with a poison tip to assassinate Rahmat Ali in Dhaka, eh? And Sammy you were the project lead on the air assault on the 'Ocean Queen' off Yemen to save the Indian Cultural Attache. We have done some incredible stuff that this country doesn't even know and all we can do is salute you. How do we get to the Chinese?"

Just at that, the conference room door buzzer went off. Kyle saw on the camera that Ct 106 was at the door.

The door swing open and CT 106 walked in with a tray of food and drinks.

In a minute, the group had devoured the chole bhatures and samosas. As the team ate, CT 106 was leaning against the main door. He cleared his throat and spoke.

"Errr sir, with permission, we could use case studies of the world wars to analyse how to grab this Chinese."

Akram was staring at CT 106.

"Aha, the man speaks, and CT 106, how the *fuck* did you know about the Chinese, eh?" Kyle glared at CT.

"Ah... err... sir! Please understand I am CT of the property. I have visual and hearing access to every part of this property that includes all rooms... *all rooms,* sir."

Akram smiled.

"Chalo, glad someone is keen to know how screwed we are! *Aap bhi bolo, mere aka.*"

"Sir, we should skydive onto the Rashtrapati Bhawan. We can use the special air infiltration suits that we used in Myanmar. Radars can't pick that up as the signals bounce off in different directions off the angular suit."

There was deathly silence in the room.

Samdup responded.

"CT, thanks, but how do we expect to get in without getting into a firefight with the PBG?"

Akram glared at CT.

"What would you like to do? Carry hakka noodles in plates acting like catering staff and kidnap the Chinese and bundle him back on to the serving plate and then walk out of RB, grab an Uber and go home? Skydive... you goddamn idiot. Sammy remind me, this asshole stays here another two years. No bloody brains!"

CT 106 was about to respond when Kyle gestured at him to stop talking.

"CT, thanks... please think through."

Norbu, who was listening reacted, "CT's plan may be tough, but in my analysis, we need to get in without getting sighted. Once in, we can lay our hands on any collateral to get out. Of course, skydiving projects on Rashtrapati Bhawan may not work as it was part of a simulation we did two years back along with Military Intelligence. We can use over ground initiative... from air seems tough, so I guess we could go under... errr..." Norbu hesitated as what he was about to say as it may just get Akram sir to strangle him.

Samdup completed his sentence.

"Dig under the structure... hilarious... thanks... so helpful. So now you want to replay the 'Great Escape' at the Rashtrapati Bhawan?"

The 'Great Escape' was a hit movie based on one of the greatest escapes from a Nazi Prison Camp. The prisoners had dug a tunnel right under the noses of the prison guards.

Samdup was now getting agitated. He knew that his brother was also part of the eighteen and he could not even imagine what he would tell his parents.

"You want to dig a bloody tunnel under the Rashtrapati Bhawan in what time frame? Two friggin' years, huh?"

Samdup looked at Akram.

"Akram, this isn't working. Let's just kidnap the CDC. Take Freddy to lure him and let's give him the the full treatment. Akram... Akram... are you listening to me?"

Samdup was looking at Akram who seemed frozen. His eyes were not blinking.

"Akram?" Samdup got up and rushed towards Akram.

As he came close, Akram sprang from his chair towards Norbu and grabbed his collar.

"Say what you just said... dig under the... *say it!*"

Norbu was in shock and whispered.

"Sorry, Sir... I was about to say that, but it's a terrible idea... Can we dig to reach the Rashtrapati Bhawan? I mean it's a silly idea..."

Akram held his face inches from Norbu.

"And you are sure Rashtrapati Bhawan was actually the Viceroy House that was in Kolkata?"

"Er... yes. That is correct, sir," Norbu was still whispering. Unsure of what Akram would do to him next.

Akram sat down and began talking to himself.

"They designed a tunnel to the Viceroy House. Your great-grandpa was a genius. Look at his picture, how handsome he looks. He was key to India's best made plan to get freedom, look at this watch..."

The team stared at Akram. Samdup was looking really concerned. Had stress got to Akram Khan? He sat next to Akram.

"Akram, Akram... hey calm down. It's fine... it will be fine. What are you saying?"

Akram looked at Samdup. He got up and gave the shocked Norbu a bear hug and then proceeded to kiss him on each cheek.

"Norbu, you useless idiot. You are a genius!"

Akram grabbed Samdup's hand.

"Come on, we need to go to Kolkata."

"Are you crazy?"

"Come on, my friend! I need to meet Didima."

CHAPTER 15
THE REVOLUTION

Kolkatta
2015

Akram and Samdup had taken the next available flight to Kolkata. Akram had called Laddoo kaka, who was Didima's Man Friday. Didima had adopted him from a local orphanage. After he finished his high school, Didima helped him set up a small tuck shop in the garage of the house. As he was not keen on higher education, he had decided to take it easy, run the tuck shop and help Didma look after the ancestral house. Akram's maternal grandmother, Didima, Mrs Sarojini Dasgupta, was now ninety-five years old. Akram's grandfather, the late Shri Sonjoy Dasgupta passed away several years back when he was only seventy-five. They had only one daughter, Akram's mother, Urvashi Dasgupta. Urvashi grew up in Kolkata, but spent almost all her growing years at their neighbour's place. The Dasguptas were an Indian Civil Services household. With a large 4800 sq yard plot in the posh Jorasanko area, the Dasguptas' neigbouring plot was owned by Nawab Ali Jamaal Khan and his large joint family. Mr Jamaal Khan had relocated his family from Hyderabad in the late 1950s. The plot was a legacy property passed onto him by one of his uncles, who he had looked after till his death.

In an environment of communal hatred and even as the embers of the partition smouldered, the Dasguptas and the

Khans had hit it off as families from day one. The fragrance of kababs on a coal spit had caught the attention of Sonjoyji on a dull Sunday morning. At lunch time, the neighbour's khansama delivered a large bowl full of shammi kebabs. The kebabs were served with some hesitation at the lunch table. Sonjoyji was known to be a fussy eater and many friendships had been sealed or broken on meal quality!

The first bite and Sonjoyji exclaimed loudly,

"Good lord! These are amazing. Food is 'sanskriti'!" he nodded at the rest of the table.

If indeed food is culture, then those kebabs were truly representative of the Indian melting pot of race, caste and religion. As is part of Indian practice, no food bowl is ever returned to a neighbour or friend empty. So, at the lord of the house's instructions, the largest possible king prawns were procured from the market and the bowl and tray was returned in the evening, brimming with the classic Dasgupta prawn curry. Food started it, but soon the families were bonding like blood relatives. Education does that sometimes. Dasgupta's only child Urvashi and the Khan's three boys became good friends. The love for English literature too helped the bonding. Both Sonjoy and Nawab sahib had been educated in England.

Many Sundays were spent in each other's living rooms, sipping sherry and recalling their days in the Queen's land! As the families bonded, it was not surprising that romance could not be too far away. Urvashi and the eldest of the Khan's siblings Amanullah or Aman Khan soon discovered their love for badminton. The large frontyard of the Dasguptas soon had a full-fledged court. The two would often practice early in the mornings. The parents were also made to understand that a morning jog was necessary to warm up. The two would often run out at 5 in the morning. The two hours they spent were all about discovering how much they enjoyed spending time with each other. In 1973, when Urvashi was twenty-five years old, the two families after a year of shock, resentment and dismay decided that the two could not find anyone better than each other. Sonjoy and Nawab sahib finally decided to raise a toast and drink to the future of the two families. The event was a quiet one, held in Darjeeling, away from prying eyes. Urvashi soon moved to Hyderabad with Aman to manage the family business of pearls. Akram was born in Hyderabad, just a year later.

Growing up in a cultural khichri was an experience in itself. Aman and Urvashi had both reached near perfect academic heights. Aman was a gemologist while Urvashi ran a school for the specially gifted in Hyderabad, after completing her post graduation from Kolkata. Learning about each other's religion had been a lesson in religious tolerance. Unfortunately, some of Aman's family had never really forgiven Nawab sahib for marrying into Hindus. In Hyderabad, Urvashi had managed to integrate so well with the Khans that often family discussions would veer towards the Hindus and Aman would deftly steer the conversation away. Urvashi knew how Aman managed that. It was another reason why she loved him so.

Tragedy befell Akram's family from his father's side. Akram's two uncles and grandparents died in a car crash in London. His cousins were scattered across the globe and he was hardly in touch with them. The Khan's property was sold off soon after the tragic accident.

***

Samdup had resisted asking too many questions. Akram seemed at a high stress level. Once they landed and were comfortably seated in a cab, Samdup put his hand on Akram's shoulder.

"Brother, what are we doing here? Are you feeling alright?"

Akram looked back at Samdup and smiled.

"I am good, Sammy. Just don't ask me more questions. I don't want to waste the time if I am wrong about this. Anyway, you haven't seen my Hindu side, have you? So enjoy meeting India's most elegant and spirited ninety-five-year-old beauty Ms Sarojini Dasgupta. She's a post-graduate in European history. Watch out, don't say anything anti-national. She's a fierce nationalist."

As Akram described his Didima, he could not help but feel the admiration and love he always had for her. Akram's mother had told her that she was the key pillar of support to allow a Hindu-Muslim marriage in those times. Interestingly, Nawab sahib had been extremely fond of Akram's mother and he was really delighted at the match.

Samdup smiled back. He would play along. Akram must know something.

As the cab trudged along the Kolkata traffic, Akram was flooded with memories of Kolkata. He knew it was a bit of a long shot, but he was dead sure that the one story of India's freedom struggle that he had Didima tell him for so many years during every summer vacation, did have some plan of an attack on the Viceroy House. He could recall words that were still imprinted in his memory. Mud displacement from tunnel digging, secret designs, and escape to Japan designed by Didima's father. He would soon put it all together.

He directed the cab to the Dasgupta residence and soon he and Samdup were standing at the main door. The residence had a huge manicured lawn, and one could see stained glass windows all around.

Laddoo kaka was at the main door and he rushed forward and enveloped Akram in a bear hug. Akram hugged back his playmate of many years.

"Akku, so glad to see you. Didima is anxiously pacing up and down. Go straight to the library."

"Laddoo kaka... *kya baat.* You are looking good. Please, please just get us some of your masala chai, please. This is my friend, Samdup."

Laddoo kaka nodded at Samdup and ushered them in.

Akram walked briskly to the library just next to the bedroom. The massive haveli would have put any British villa to shame. With a large hall, kitchen, bedroom and library on the ground floor, it had seven bedrooms on the first floor.

The library, as Akram recalled, was a beautiful design of teak wood and housed almost 1800 books. He could still almost smell the leather on the easy chairs in the middle and the well-stocked bar in the corner.

They had just reached the main door when Samdup set his eyes for the first time on Akram's grandmother Ms Sarojini Dasgupta.

Clad in a beautiful Kantha stich silk saree, her grey hair looked just right on her wrinkled face. She was gorgeous, like a movie star of the yesteryears.

Akram ran and hugged her.

"Didima!"

"Hmm, so my Akki finally remembered that his didima is still alive. Eh, two years and no word!" As she spoke, she was planting kiss after kiss on Akram and holding his face in her hands.

"Hmmm... so dry... and wrinkles already. Come... come, let's settle down, handsome."

Didima paused to look at Samdup.

"Meet Samdup, my office colleague and dear friend," Akram told her.

Didima smiled at Samdup, "Welcome! Welcome!"

All three grabbed the beautiful easy chairs around the small centre table.

Samdup looked around the library. It was indeed very impressive. Leather bound books in teakwood cabinets from floor to ceiling. It was sheer opulence. He never knew Akram had such rich heritage!

"So Akku, what's happening? Is there some conference happening, my dear?"

"Didima, you know I work with various departments of the government, looking at different aspects. We are now doing some archiving work for the government regarding British history and I recalled all the lovely stories you narrated to me. I thought Sammy and I could come here and just take your inputs... eh... right Sammy,right?

"Err... umm yes. Archiving work that needed some more... umm... information."

Didima looked at both of them and smiled.

"I may be ninety-five years, my dear Akku, but these hands have washed your naked bum for years, so don't you go about telling me all this nonsense about archives. You must have reasons to hide the truth from me, so I will not pester you. You could have well asked me for 'inputs' over the phone, but you're here, so it must be something really important to you. Right?"

Akram looked down at his feet in embarrassment. She was just too bloody sharp. What an asset she would been in intelligence gathering, he thought to himself.

"Didima... I... I don't know what to say. Yes, it is very important, so I want you to share everything you can about that story you told me about the Indian freedom struggle and the Viceroy House and something you used to say about digging tunnels in Japan or was it Kolkata—"

Didima cut him off.

"Ooof Baba, slowly slowly. I get it."

Ladoo kaka entered the library with a large tray laden with chai and food. Samdup looked at the tray and realised that they had not eaten in quite a while.

"First we will eat, and then I will tell you all about your great country, eh. Laddoo, sweety, go run to the store and get my leather bag, will you? The one with the number lock on it. Quickly!"

While Akram and Samdup gorged on the fantastic array of sweets and savouries, Laddoo kaka returned and placed a large leather suitcase on the side chair.

Didima eased into the large leather chair and having sunk in, she looked at the ceiling. She closed her eyes, held her hands together placing them in her lap and started her narrative of an amazing history lesson that not too many Indians knew about.

"Akki, it was always my dream that you became an architect. But you were just too sports loving, no? *Bodmash*, I tried impressing upon your mother, but you know how free-spirited my Urvashi is, right! Your great grandfather Shri Prodipto Sengupta was one of the finest architects in the commonwealth... eh... I bet you didn't understand what that meant. You were with me only during summer, no? When I was just eight years old, he would teach me design concepts that he had thought of and he would make miniature models with matchsticks. In the 1900s, Bengal was the hotbed of freedom fighters. What the British did to Bengal was enough to make the Bengalis rise in anger. What was also clear was that the freedom movement in Bengal was not aligned to the Congress's non-violent movement. We felt..."

Akram noticed the word 'we' that Didma used. Akram was sure that Didima too played some role in India's freedom movement. He noticed Samdup deep in concentration, one eyebrow twitching with nervousness. He smiled and came back to Didima's narration.

"...felt that we had been butchered and the British had been merciless. Turn the other cheek was hardly what the average Bengali wanted to do. Do you recall the Anushilan Samiti, Akki?"

Before Akram could respond, Didima continued.

"The samiti was the base of the very thought of a violent uprising. The approach was that the British will only leave in fear, never otherwise. The Ghosh brothers – Harobindo and

Biru were the first movers. Scheming, planning small attacks with home-made bombs was just the beginning. Imagine their vision when using the Indian diaspora in Britain, they established connections with the governments in France, Turkey and Japan. Support was forthcoming in the form of funds as well as equipment. A lot of training was given by the French, first in France and then by sending trainers into French colonies."

Akram was astounded with this narrative. He could hardly remember any of it.

"And Didima, you mean your Baba was part of our freedom movement?"

"Uffff, you are still so impatient, no? My baba was a fantastic architect. In fact, he was handpicked by Sir Lutyens to help him in India. What I know from my mother was that initially he was just Sahib bahadur, the typical Bengali British Sahib. You know what I am saying, right? Studied in Britain, erudite, trying to be one of them, eh?"

Didima looked at Samdup. "Do you know what I am saying, young man?"

Samdup responded with a smile, "Of course, Didima. My growing up years were in Darjeeling, so I know exactly what you are saying."

Didima smiled and continued.

"Well, so Baba came to India after being appointed to the team of designers that set up office in India. His only connection to the freedom movement was just what he read in the newspapers or from gossip. You should know that for the average Bengali in those days, an English education was just non-negotiable if one was to make a mark in society. One of his closest friends in UK was Hargobind Ghosh. History has been unkind to the Bengali revolutionaries. You may know him as Shri Harobindo Ghosh who set up an ashram in Pondicherry."

"Of course, Didima. I know the ashram. We even visited it many years back. Remember, you were not able to travel, so we just went and stayed in Pondicherry for a week. But I didn't know the connection to the freedom movement. We also read of the Holy Mother, who I think was French and came to help with the spiritual movement."

Didima stared at Akram and it seemed that she was hesitating to share something.

Akram noticed that. "Didima, I am right?"

"Akki, well... maybe ten percent right with whatever British historians want you to believe. Aah, if I had the energy, I would write a book. After being jailed, Harobindo did have some kind of a spiritual experience, but for him, India's freedom was equally critical. So, after his release he ran off to a French colony where the French government already knew of him. They helped him set up place there. His initial plan was to drive the movement from Pondicherry. They would train our freedom fighters in the skill sets needed for a guerrilla style warfare. Misha Waseel was a French-born political activist. Trained in the craft she was also an occultist and had had visions of an Asiatic figure who she would collaborate with. In 1914, she joined Harobindo in Pondicherry and was also influenced by his spiritual force. For sometime, they did train a few Indian revolutionaries, but then decided to move to Japan to help with the Indian National Army and S.C. Bose. But let me not digress, that's another story. Baba, being friends with Harobindo as well as his closest friend Prabal, was slowly motivated to join the Anushilan Samiti. But my Maa told me that she was the real reason why Baba forayed into the freedom struggle. Your great grandmother was Pavitra, my baba's closest friend, Prabal's sister. She was a firebrand revolutionary, always stepping up to take charge. Anyway, so Baba was a reluctant freedom fighter!"

With this, Didima let out a loud giggle and grabbed some masala peanuts from the tray.

Didima noticed that it had been two hours already, "Ohhh, it's late. Should we have something to eat?"

"No... no Didima, please tell us more. What happened to the Viceroy House? I recall you told me Baba had bombed the Viceroy or attacked him or something?"

"Uff, impatient again!" She playfully reached out to Akram's ear and gently pulled it.

"I told you how my mother persuaded Baba to join the samiti, no? So, the samiti members were nursing their wounds after their bombing initiatives were failing. Take the Alipore case. Instead of killing the evil magistrate, the bomb landed in the wrong carriage and two innocent British women died. Members were keen to plan something really big and that 'big' was to assassinate the Viceroy of India."

Samdup could not help but sit up in awe at this story. His mouth was already open. "Oh my lord!"

Samdup could tell that Akram got his storytelling genes from Didima. She was a fantastic raconteur.

Akram was equally in shock. His bloodline was of such brave folks. He swelled with pride and he now knew that his fierce love for his country was truly in his blood.

"The only challenge was how to get it done. The British security apparatus was impressive. They had informers all over. A large part of the police force was also native Indian and they could easily infiltrate samiti members. That's how they caught the planners of the Alipore bomb scandal. Just when Baba took charge of his position in Kolkata, Prabal inducted him into the samiti. Soon, he was part of planning small actions. Also the romance of Baba and Ma blossomed at the Ekla café."

With this, Didima opened her suitcase and picked out an 8 inch by 6 inches photograph of three Indians. Akram saw the photograph. "Aaah, you gave me a copy, Didima. This is Baba, Boro Maa and her brother Prabal uncle, right??

Didima fondly grabbed Akram's hands and nodded, "Indeed. And look, in the background is Ekla Café."

Samdup jumped up to get a closer look.

"Baba and Ma. Beautiful couple, no? Anyway, the samiti members planned and planned. From bombs to poisonous snakes, but nothing seemed to be working. In any case, the British government was also moving the seat of power to Delhi. Baba was sent to India precisely to work on plans that Sir Lutyens was making along with another senior architect named Baker. It was in one of the coffee sessions, that Maa told me, your Baba came up with a fantastic plan of assassinating the Viceroy. He discussed this with the team and the plan was as incredible in vision, as simple it was in execution."

Akram sat up straight as his memories came flooding back. It was now so familiar.

"Baba would design a pit near the Viceroy House for an explosive device that we set off with the pressure of the carriage wheels, right Didima?"

"Of course not! What are you saying Akki? Here, look at this! Then you will understand."

Didima opened the suitcase and after rummaging about for a bit, drew out a plastic folder. From the folder she extracted a laminated sheet that she handed to Akram. Samdup stood up and walked to Akram's chair and both of them saw the paper that appeared to be a rather official looking letter.

In Service of the British Centre for Design and Construction
The India office, INDIA

1913, 10th Day February

For
The Honourable Chief Engineer
Sir Henry Margot, Delhi

Draft Roll Design 42/132/1912

It is my privilege to advise you that draft design has met with approval in the central committee meeting held in London last month. Kindly begin with the Tender process to acquire material and staff. An additional cost of Pound Sterling 8000 is earmarked for an additional structure change. Estimate calculations are appended for the 'King's Escape' as requested for and approved by the Committee under the Leadership of Sir Lutyens.

The latest draft design has been marked for the structure as well as ingress-egress of the new structure.

We graciously seek your approval to begin work now that Committee has granted approval.

In Her Majesty's Service
Prodipto Sengupta
On behalf of the Master Designer India

CHAPTER 16
THE HISTORY OF OUR FUTURE

Kolkatta
2015

As Akram and Samdup spent time staring at the piece of history, they realised what a treasure of information Didima had. She certainly should have written a book. One could see the rich texture of the paper and the exquisite handwriting. The paper had aged and had a yellow rust base, but the lamination had helped arrest the ageing. This was part of our history that any museum would be proud to possess.

Akram was awestruck. “This was written by Baba. I don’t recall ever seeing this, Didima.”

“Yes, my dear. It is too sensitive to share with everyone. What happened later is indeed a little tragic, so I don’t like to share this often.”

Samdup reacted, “What happened later? Please do share. I am grateful that you think I am worthy of sharing this information with.”

Didima looked at Samdup. “Son, anyone that my Akki trusts, I trust.”

Laddoo kaka had laid out some food. Didima claimed she was not hungry. While Akram and Samdup ate, Akram could not hold himself back.

“Didima, but tell me what happened to Baba. I still don’t understand this letter. But how come the family never discussed this?”

"You will understand, Akki. Soon you will understand. The plan was to build a tunnel under the Viceroy House in Delhi, or Rashtrapati Bhawan, as it is called now under the guise of what is called a 'King's escape'. This was a standard practice to have escape routes for important government heads akin to those in castles. The plan was approved, ingeniously planned by Baba. Built by the British. The escape route was a tunnel right under the master bedroom of the Viceroy to about a mile out to where India Gate is today."

As he heard the words Rashtrapati Bhawan and tunnel, Samdup jumped up from the chair.

"Holy fuck! Your Baba built a tunnel under the Rashtrapati Bhawan. Fuck! Fuck!"

Samdup was shouting at Akram and rushed to give him a sloppy bear hug.

Akram hugged him back and hushed him to calm down.

"Sorry... sorry Didima. I... sorry..."

Didima was smiling.

"Well, am glad someone is so delighted with what my Baba did. Must be something important for the two of you, I guess, far more than the tall story that Akki told his Didima... huh?"

Akram smiled back. "Didima you are right. The truth is that I can't share everything with you. It's a matter of national security, but you are already so helpful. Just tell me was this plan ever executed?"

"Executed, my dear? Such tough language. The honest answer is I don't know. All we do know is that the plan was approved and sent to the engineering division. The construction, I am told, was delayed by almost six years, so the samiti dropped the plans to use the tunnel."

Akram was now curious. "But then how come no one talks about this. It would be a fantastic tourist attraction?"

"Well, you see Akki, this was a top secret development. I am quite sure that there must have been protocols to keep it a secret. Perhaps it never got made."

"But Didima, when did Baba retire from the service?"

Didima looked at Akki.

"He never retired, Akki. Prabal, my uncle and Baba's best friend was arrested by the police in 1921. Thanks to an informant, they raided the warehouse of Ekla Café and found a cache of arms. Of the documents recovered from him, some were notes made by Pavitra maa. Just as the police had informers, the samiti too had informers inside the police. They got word that warrants were being issued for Pavitra and Prodipto Sengupta. One of the key revolutionaries was a weapons expert who played a key role in setting up the INA in Germany with Netaji. He was headed to Japan with the help of Misha Waseel in Pondicherry. Maa and Baba were smuggled out of Calcutta along with him and the three escaped to Japan. Baba's sister was sadly arrested and she died of a heart attack even before she reached jail. I was then born in Tokyo three years later. We sought refuge and stayed in Tokyo till 1932 and then managed to return to Pondicherry. Baba worked with Sri Harobindo in the Ashram and the Mother. He owed their lives to them. Baba passed away in 1940, not able to see a free India. and Maa and I returned to Kolkata."

Akram and Samdup were tongue tied at this saga. Akram had never really realised his heritage and the awe-inducing adventure of his great-grandfather. The Ekla Café photograph would now have a new perspective and he was dying to share this with his wife and daughter. Akram shook himself out of his thoughts. A problem needed resolution first.

"Didima, is there any further communication that you have on this king's escape?"

"Akki, there are a lot of papers in here. Many years back I took them out and had them laminated. Here is the full suitcase. I am now feeling exhausted. It's my bedtime. You have a go and we'll meet in the morning."

Didima got up and hugged Akram and gave him a big kiss on the forehead. As she walked away, Samdup looked at Akram and remarked,

"You and I have done some pretty remarkable stuff in our lives, Akki, but I don't think it will even come close to what we heard today. A real pity India did not unravel the British historians' bias. Incredible – an Indian architect gets Sir Lutyens to approve of a tunnel to be used for the Indian freedom struggle!"

"Sammy, we don't know if it ever got built, but you know that I am clutching at straws now. Come on, we've got work to do."

He heard a cough from the main door and saw Laddoo kaka at the door. "I am making a pot of masala chai for you. Will leave it on the table."

"Thanks, Laddoo kaka."

Akram grabbed the suitcase and placed it on the main study table.

After two hours, Akram and Samdup had sorted all the papers and classified and indexed them. There were some personal letters, some related to business and property. There was some communication about Baba sending a letter that was returned by Indian post. It was a resignation letter. There was a design draft roll with the Rashtrapati Bhawan's designs with several hand markings. It was incredible to see the basic design of the Rashtrapati Bhawan with the carriageway from the main building and the green all around. There were even the four fountains designed that stood around the India Gate.

There was no mention of the king's escape in any more communication.

Akram gave out a frustrated sigh. "Bloody hell. Nothing! So we are totally screwed. Sammy, you found something?" Akram was flipping over pages.

"No Akki, nothing."

It was almost midnight. Akram suddenly saw Laddoo kaka enter the library with a tray full of tea and some more food.

"You boys must be tired."

"Arre Laddoo kaka, you are a lifesaver. In fact, Kaka, we were just thinking of heading back to the airport. There is a 5 a.m. Air India flight to Delhi and we must get back."

"Didima said to wake her if you leave. She said you were not to go without meeting her."

Akram nodded and got up and headed to the bedroom next to the kitchen

The door was slightly ajar and Akram pushed the door to find Didima in a sitting posture in bed, with a pillow behind her back.

"Arre, Didima, why aren't you asleep?"

"Akki, when my child is worried to death, how can I get sleep? I know you work for the government and there is something you are looking for and so important that you came all the way to Kolkata. Maybe this old woman can help you. Tell me and I will try and see if I can help you."

Akram stared at Didima and thought to himself, "Balls to the official secrets act!"

"Didima, we need access to the Rashtrapati Bhawan. I can't tell you the details. All I can promise you is that I will never harm a single Indian national, but my team is in trouble and I need to do this."

Didima held Akram's face in her hands and whispered,

"Akram Khan, you are the great-grandson of an Indian freedom fighter. Loyalty to your nation is in your blood and if you must do this, then you should do this."

Akram could feel his eyes well up and he turned away in a moment of awkwardness.

"As to access to the Viceroy... sorry... Rashtrapati Bhawan is concerned, I really can't say I recall this, but I must tell you that even when we were in Tokyo, Baba would love playing design puzzles. He would make structures of various kinds and then ask me to make them collapse by merely removing one matchstick. So naughty, he was, my baba!"

"Didima, think... think. Did he ever show you the path on the draft design? There is one detailed plan. But I can't see any structure of the tunnel."

Didima was in deep thought and was murmuring to herself.

"No, Akki. I can't recall. I am old, you know. Am sorry, darling. I can't remember anything else."

"Then what should I do? Dig up all around the Rashtrapati Bhawan with 150 diggers, eh?"

Akram just realised what he had said and hugged Didima.

"Sorry Maa, I just don't know what to do. Can I carry your suitcase with me to Delhi? I will get my friends to look through it again."

"Akki, it's yours. Baba would have been proud that he could do something for you."

Didima walked Akram out to the hall where Sammy was already waiting with the suitcase in his hand. Akram looked at him quizzicaly.

"Sorry, I am sure you would have taken Didima's permission, right?"

Akram nodded. He turned and hugged Didima.

Samdup came up to Didima said, "I am proud that I met you today. It was really my honour."

As the trio walked to the door, Samdup noticed that the living room was full of paintings, but the common theme seemed to be the lotus flower.

"Beautiful paintings. Did you paint them? Whoever did, really loved the lotus flower!"

Didima looked around the room.

"Well, it was my Maa. Baba always told her that he was always inspired by the lotus. You do know that Sarojini also means 'a pond full of lotus flowers'. Baba was always so in love with the flower. He said the lotus symbolises purity and beauty, even when you are surrounded by an unseemly environment."

When they reached the main door, Akram turned around.

"Thank you, Maa."

"Akki, I'm sorry I was of little help. Baba used to say that he learnt the true power of the lotus in Japan as the Japanese taught him that Lord Buddha said that he was like the lotus flower. Grown in mud but showing the way to beauty. I pray that Lord Buddha and the lotus flower show you the way, my son."

With this, Didima turned and walked away from the main door.

Akram stared at her receding figure. "What a woman, my Didima," he muttered.

Laddoo kaka had offered to drive them to the airport and as they got into the car he noticed, even in the dark of the night, the small pond in the main porch with lotuses.

He smiled. Well, even he had never noticed the lotuses. Sammy was bloody sharp, he thought.

As they drove out of the compound and took a turn, Samdup was shocked when Akram suddenly grabbed Laddoo kaka's arm and shouted.

"Holy bloody fuck! Turn the car! *Turn the car, kaka... now!*"

Laddoo kaka nearly drove the car into a divider in fright.

"What *re*? What happened?"

"Turn the car, Kaka... Now please!"

Akram was panicking. "Bloody hell! How did we miss it? The bastard had it there all the time. We just didn't notice it!"

"Akram, what are you talking about? What the hell is happening?"

"Sammy, you friggin genius! I think you just solved it."

Once they reached the house, Akram ran inside. "Sammy, get the draft out of the suitcase and spread it on the dining table. Hurry!"

Akram ran at a sprint to Didima's room.

"Didima, just come to the dining room... *now! Please!*"

Didima was shocked at Akram's return. What had come over this young man?

"Ufff, re... What happened? You're back?"

Akram grabbed her by her arm and they walked to the dining table. Sammy had already spread the one and only draft design roll onto the table. The designs were very detailed and had markings in different colours.

"Now Didima, you told me that Baba was very fond of the lotus flower."

"Yes, so?"

"When I saw the drawing, I noticed that at many places, Baba had used motifs on flowers. Like small sunflowers just to show a green patch, etc. Notice the big patch just adjacent to the main structure."

He placed his index finger and they all stared down at the design.

"Here is what we now know as the Mughal Gardens. Look at various motifs used. Can you spot any lotus?

Meanwhile, Laddoo kaka had managed to procure a large magnifying glass and gave it to Didima.

"No, no lotuses here."

"Isn't it odd that an ace designer who so loved the lotus hasn't used the lotus anywhere in the designs?"

"Yes Akki, it is strange. But what do you mean?"

"I mean, Didima, that since this tunnel was his brainchild, he must have used some code to highlight the placement of the tunnel."

Didima looked at him, “Hmmm, yes, you have a point. Oh my god! All you have to do is find the lotus flowers!”

Akram stood up straight and yelled, “Yes! Yes! It has to be that. Give me that magnifying glass, damn it!”

As the others stood aside, Akram bent over the canvas and started sweeping the entire structure for a lotus flower.

Almost ten minutes had passed and no lotus. Could Akram be wrong?

The first spotting was made by Samdup without any magnifying glass. He was pondering that if he wanted to make a tunnel, he would make it where one would least expect it. As he peered closely behind the estate boundary of the structure, he spotted a tiny speck of pink on the canvas.

“MG, please.”

Akram handed him the magnifying glass and moved next to Sammy.

“Mmmmmm, Akram ji. You are a bloody genius, man! It’s there... the most miniature of gorgeous pink lotuses. I have found the line. All we have to do is start tracing it. Get a pencil, quick.”

After almost an hour. Akram and Samdup had traced a line from the rear side of the structure, going alongside the boundary walls, straight towards what is the main drive from the RB to where the India Gate is located at present. At both ends of the line were obviously the ingress and egress gates in form of symbols of a cluster of lotus flowers so small that it was just a speck to the naked eye.

Didima got up from the chair, patted Akram’s hand. “You’ve done it, Akki. I am proud of you. Now I am retiring. I suggest you get some rest and catch a later flight.”

Eyes bloodshot with the strain, Didima turned and walked to her bedroom. Laddoo kaka too had probably gone off as well. Samdup and Akram stood back and stared at their two hours of work.

"He was a genius, Sammy. Just see how it traces along with boundary walls. The base structure would help form a support to one side of the tunnel, so all you have to do is reinforce only one side. So he must have communicated the same code somehow to the engineering department."

Samdup looked at the canvas, "Akki, remember we still don't know if it was constructed. We are merely guessing that it was."

"My friend, this design is made to scale. See that scale reference at the bottom. So, all we have to do now is find the gate at the end that is away from the bhawan. If we can find that, we can be sure it was made... right?"

"Right. So we go to Delhi. Take a few excavators and start digging near one of the most secure locations in the country... huh?"

Akram shook his head, "You're such a worry curry! We'll find a way, buddy. Let's just catch some sleep."

Akram took the large sofa in the library and Samdup chose the carpet on the floor.

Akram went off to sleep almost as soon as he lay down. He felt enormous relief almost like the lifting of a big burden from his head. We have a chance now, he thought. We have a chance.

CHAPTER 17
DEATH OF A PATRIOT

New Delhi
2015

It was Sunday and the Chinese delegation was to arrive in four days' time.

As they flew back home, they maintained a stoic silence. The moot point was – what after they find the structure? Were they, an Indian RAW team, prepared to break into the Rashtrapati Bhawan, break through the last security detail, inflict some violence, grab hold of the Chinese delegate, neutralise his personal security and then finally what? Akram and Samdup were seasoned professionals and they were already estimating various scenarios and collateral damages for each scenario.

What happens after they kidnap the Chinese delegate? How would the Indian government react? Finally, this would be seen and labelled as a terrorist attack. Indeed there was a high probability that the last security cordon would be able to neutralise the raiding party by simply taking them out. The special forces were more than special. Each was a handpicked warrior.

Engrossed in their thoughts, time flew and soon they were waving to Norbu who had come to pick them up.

"Akki, I think this will be a suicide mission. We will never take counter measures against our forces, but they will see us as terrorists. I think we are planning a raid that will have only one consequence – failure."

Akram knew that Samdup was right. Even if they were able to crack the exit, what next? Who would organise a raiding party on the Rashtrapati Bhawan? A team of RAW agents! Or should he look at recruiting 'Freelance artists (FLAs)'. FLAs were essentially trained men who were either part of an organised criminal group or even part of the armed forces of a country. They were either laid off, had a minor mobility medical challenge or simply did not qualify to continue. Indian intelligence network had a full database of FLAs and RAW had often used them in foreign countries. Akram had personally used them in Russia as well as Nepal. Neutralising some entities who were clearly anti-India was an important part of foreign policy.

Not commonly known was an ugly truth, that in Nepal, Bangladesh and even Myanmar. Indian foreign policy often used RAW operations to compromise individuals who were clearly anti-India. Instruments were mostly honey traps where they were offered sexual favours and then filmed. One of RAW's successful operations in Sri Lanka involved kidnapping the target, filming him in a homosexual act in a manner that the viewer could not make out that the target was drugged and then blackmailing him or releasing the footage to a media house. This operation was most useful in Islamic countries and India had great success in Iran with a similar operation. Other instruments ranged from kidnapping family members to occasionally terminating the target. Akram knew that while anonymity was an advantage of FLAs, unpredictable behaviour was a big disadvantage. FLAs lacked discipline and would sometimes mess up the operation.

"Norbu, let's head to the holhome. What is happening there?"

Before Norbu could response, Akram's phone buzzed. It was Freddy.

"Hi Freddy!"

"Where the hell have you been? Have been trying your bloody phone for more than 24 hours?" Akram, use the drop site, access the document. Reach the guesthouse asap. We need to meet."

"Noted. ETA eighteen minutes."

Akram nodded to Samdup. "Access the drop site, send everything to Kyle, ask him to be ready. Team meeting in eighteen minutes."

Samdup nodded back and went to work on his phone.

"So Norbu, what were you saying?"

"Sir, I... nothing sir, I was just saying that our team is getting bored. We were prepped for action, but the gear is not of any use. We should discuss what we do next. Full gear and forty hours with no communication makes them impatient."

Akram nodded. "Soon enough. Please stay in full gear. We will decide today. By the way, please acquire from the armoury, the sound and light blanks we had used for training. Please replace all real ammo with the play blanks, right now. But your team should not know we have done this."

Norbu stared at Akram and then Samdup.

"I..." and then training took over. "Noted sir, will be done in two hours."

Samdup knew exactly what was happening. Akram would never ever even think of harming a single fellow Indian.

He was making sure that there was no accident during the operation. He knew that soon enough, Akram would also have Norbu remove the armed combat weapons that the RAW protection teams had on their body armour. It was just an incredible situation.

On their arrival at the safe house, Akram and Samdup found Freddy and Kyle already waiting for them in the conference room. Akram could not but glance again at the main screen which still continued to have eighteen blinking red lights. A reminder to the team of their brave colleagues now in custody in China, hopefully still alive.

Freddy got up and grabbed Akram's shoulder, "How are you holding up, Akram? You fine?"

Freddy was genuine in his concern. Whatever was in the past, it was in the past. Akram had realised that Freddy was only a victim of being part of the rat race of recognitions and positions as a bureaucrat.

"All okay, Freddy...what's happening?"

"Happening?" Freddy exclaimed. "More than happening, buddy. Look what I have for you."

With a flourish, Freddy extracted sheets from his hand bag and kept them on the table one at a time.

It was a 'Guest Protection Programme – Liu Ronji' document.

Akram and Samdup were amazed and stared at Freddy in awe. The GPP was the standard process guide for all super VIP events. It laid down minute by minute activity list of the guest and responsibility on who was doing what. It was drawn to minute detail as much as what colour clothes will our dignitaries be wearing and what colour clothes will the guest be wearing. In the event of an action, events happen at a very fast pace and sometimes colours are critical to help protection detail act to protect the guest. Often, one notices dignitaries wearing lapel pins of their home country. These are radio frequency markers that are important markers for snipers. When you are 800 metres away, you need a technology patch to help you ensure that no one gets hurt in friendly fire.

"Freddy, these are counted and scanned for source. You do know what happens if it gets out that we had access to this document."

"Akram, either I am in or I am not in. I know what's happening buddy. We have to get our team back and we need to take this Chinese guy into our custody. I do know you have Kyle, who is the best asset to run this snatch, so I can make out what's happening here. Frankly, now I don't care. I cannot live with the fact that I may have caused harm to come to our agents in China. I would rather be hanged for treason."

It was now 48 hours to the Rashtrapati Bhawan meeting of the Indian President and Prime minister, along with Liu Ronji. It appeared that Ronji had spent time in India as a student when his father was posted to the Delhi embassy and had gone to school along with the President of India's son-in-law. Just as luck would have it, Ronji had sought to also meet the President and hence the meeting venue had shifted to the Rashtrapati Bhawan.

"Okay Freddy, this is bloody good work. Impressive, Sirji, impressive."

Akram nodded at Kyle. "Okay K, action time, get Norbu in."

Norbu and Kyle came back in a minute.

Taking a long deep breath, Akram sat down on the table and began what he had not done in some years – a Preop briefing to the team. Preop, or Pre-operations briefing was given by the main sponsor of any operation. It set objectives, ingress-egress routes, how important was the successful outcome of the mission and how should the team prioritise in case things go bad.

Staring at Kyle and Norbu, Akram began his briefing. Kyle had already prepared a dossier of information related to the Op. Kyle nodded to Norbu and soon Norbu's six team members joined the meeting. Unlike armed forces operations, smaller groups require a common briefing rather than only to the team leader. Norbu's chosen six protection details were a mix of Indian-born Tibetan origin and special RAW protection force members. Samdup had discussed and thought this through. Any such action would have to be a small team. There was no time now to rustle up a large team as in any case, their limiting condition was not to harm any fellow Indians. Norbu knew that Samdup would also take away small weapons for hand-to-hand combat like the five-inch Kimoro blades.

"Well, eighteen of our team members are in custody of the Chinese government. This has happened on account of an action by our government of cosying up to the Chinese. They have, by a devious action, stolen the A list. Our objective is to capture a senior ranking member of the Chinese government who is here on a secret visit to sign a deal. We will use him as collateral and get our colleagues. This will involve mounting an operation on our own soil at a government building. *But* we will not harm in any way *any* of our fellow Indians. However, they will see us as hostile and may take action to thwart our efforts. This is a unique operation. Your hands are tied behind your back. It is certain some of us may get injured or captured. If you don't feel committed to this operation, step back now."

Akram stared at the team in the room. He knew that the spirit of devotion to one's nation was a driver for many, but in this situation, how do you react when your own government was the enemy. Was it the nation state or was it the leader of the nation's ruling party that was the enemy?

"Earlier I gave instructions to Norbu to surreptitiously change your munition to blanks, but I feel we must be transparent that I do not want any shots fired even by accident.

"We are not yet certain of ingress-egress routes, but we have information that will give us a safe access to the target.

"Norbu will explain the operation in detail after Kyle hands out the full plan. We will move the Chinese guest to another location that I have already authorised. We will ensure no harm will come to our Chinese guest. Please remember, the Chinese is not the enemy today. This briefing is over."

As Norbu and team marched out, Freddy put his arm around Samdup.

"Samdup, this is a very impressive team you have put together. I know Akram deserves all the applause, but I know the silent worker behind the scenes, eh?"

Samdup was surprised at this show of affection. He guessed that Akram may have been right. Freddy was on their side.

Akram turned to Freddy.

"Freddy, you have already taken a lot of risk. You should now leave. I want to ensure you have deniability if things sour out and..."

Freddy cut him with a brisk wave of his hand in the air.

"Akram, shut up. I may be an old foggie. I am totally in now. You know you need my brains, right?" he smiled at Akram.

As espionage required acute presence of mind and higher than average IQ, RAW ran several tests to fit agents into the structure. Freddy had a Score of 131, that made him part of the world's top two percent population. For this reason, Freddy was a sought after talent in Analytics, Scenario building and even at Agent placement.

Akram smiled back, "That I do need, Freddy. You're in. Gentlemen, we now have less than 35 hours. We now have to determine where is the ingress-egress point of the tunnel."

"Tunnel?" Freddy exclaimed. "What bloody tunnel?"

Akram briefed Freddy on the developments of the last forty-eight hours.

"Akram, this has to be the most incredible yarn you have spun or an incredible part of our history that no one has recorded. You mean we had built a tunnel to assassinate the Viceroy? Hell! Amazing! Lets see the drafts then..."

Samdup rolled open the designs.

Samdup took a laser pointer and started showing the pink lotus line to Freddy and Akram.

"So, here it is... exits from the rear and then traces along with the external boundary wall and runs straight up towards, what ought to be... err... what... I think India Gate?"

The design had no mention of the India Gate as that came up much later in the plans.

Freddy remarked, "This is bloody detailed, man. It's drawn to scale... see below!"

Using a pencil, Freddy converted the pencil to a scale measurement reference tool. And soon, using the length of the pencil, had already measured the distance from the entrance of the Rashtrapati Bhawan to the apparent exit point of the tunnel.

"This looks to be about 1.6 kilometres from the main entrance. And it looks just off to the left from the main carriageway. You see that? It's somewhere in the lawns. How can that be? You can't have the exit covered in mud and grass and soon over years layer on layer of mud will be laid making the exit totally inoperational. If it's not in the lawns, where can it be?"

Akram stared at the design. "Kyle, access aerial view please... let's see."

Kyle pulled up a satellite imagery of the latest shots from the Israeli satellite.

"All right, so here we are. Kyle, can you use the scale on the design draft and place it on top of the sat image on scale."

Kyle tool out his phone camera and clicked a picture of the draft and then importing it on the main server he had already managed to match scale of the two images.

"Right! So here is the design canvas image."

As he spoke, a picture of the design made by Akram's great-grandfather appeared on the screen.

"...and here is the satellite image fitted to scale of the design canvas. I adjusted the height of the picture to match the scale. I have marked the lotus line with a red marker... line... there. Can you see it?"

With this, another image appeared right on top of the design almost like a watermark and all could see the sharp redline. It was incredible to see a design made in the early 1900s and a satellite image more than a hundred years later.

Freddy picked up the laser marker. And traced the red maker line.

"Hmm... so here we are... it ends here... and the satellite image has a..."

Everyone strained to see the satellite image.

"Friggin hell, it's near the fountain next to the India Gate. Is it under the bloody water body? We are screwed then."

Akram stared at the picture. "We have less than eighteen hours now. It's 4 p.m. We need to find the damn exit."

Samdup had already stood up. "We need a site inspection. Now!"

Freddy and Akram nodded and in minutes they were bundled up in a car and tearing away to India Gate. Bengali Market was but two kilometres away, so it took them just eight minutes and they were already at the site.

Kyle had grabbed a 'tool kit' as he left the safe house. The tool kit was a RAW's operative standard issue set of craft tools. From eavesdropping bugs to some spy cameras and lock picks, it also had a density metric tool that used ultrasound waves to determine the material and density of any matter it bounced against. For instance, it could measure how thick the walls were, were they concrete or brick or metal? Were they hollow? When searching for documents and hiding places, it was of enormous help.

When they arrived at the fountain, they were not surprised to see a motley crowd of families who had come to have a quiet evening. Street vendors moved around. Finding the fountain, the four quickly decided to find a spot near the fountain. Freddy took charge of the search and divided the area around the fountain into four sectors. They knew they stood out in the crowd, four men moving around in a strange way, but they didn't care.

Freddy, using a broken branch, drew the sectors on the ground, allocating the sectors. They had to look for a possible pathway made almost a hundred years ago that led to the tunnel.

As they took the sectors allocated to them, they knew they had to find something out of place, but it was also possible that years of plant growth and refreshing the ground with fresh mud may have put in at least a feet of ground soil on top of any exit.

An hour passed and there was nothing that anyone could identify.

Akram shrugged his hands in despair.

"Could the damn fountains have covered it?"

Freddy nodded, "Yes, that's a possibility and there's no way we can tear apart the damn fountain in such little time."

"Though Akram, I am wondering that if this freedom fighter dude was top of his class, etc, and so bloody good, he would have designed something to make sure it would not have got covered with a bloody concrete fountain, no? We are just missing it. You are missing it in your sectors."

Kyle stared at the team and spoke, "I think the red stone fountain is the only structure built for longevity. No one would just create a trap door and leave it to be discovered or just cover it with ground soil. Let's split up the fountain and focus on it."

Freddy nodded, "Kyle the smartie has spoken, huh? And I agree with his assessment. It's in the damn fountain. Gentlemen, we have to get *inside* the fountain." With this, Freddy had taken off his shoes and was rolling up his trousers.

Soon, Freddy and Kyle had climbed into the fountain while Akram and Samdup were scanning the outside perimeter of the fountain. It was an odd sight to see two men inside the fountain, peering at the bottom.

Another eighteen minutes passed and the team was now losing confidence.

Akram shouted across the fountain, "Nothing at all?"

The other three shook their heads and Freddy shouted back, "Nothing inside the damn fountain. Your great-grandad should have used a bloody flag marker, man. Who hides an exit so well that no one can bloody find it, eh?"

"Flag marker?" Samdup yelled. "Flag marker! Oh god, we are so stupid, Akram! What if he had a chance to even plan the fountain that may have come later... eh... then we already know his flag marker...right? Akram?"

Akram stared back at Samdup and suddenly yelled in excitement as all four suddenly shouted in unison.

"A pink lotus!"

The team went back to work.

It was a mere three minutes later when both Akram and Samdup shouted almost together.

"Something here... Come on, get out of the fountain, you two!"

Akram had found on the baseline of the outer perimeter of the fountain a small grid at the bottom of the red stone fountain base. A thin line of engravings of the lotus could be seen with the visible eye. It ran for almost eight feet and formed a rectangle on the fountain wall that was almost 8*2 feet in height. Right at the centre was a large engraving of a lotus flower that was not there at any other place in the fountain.

All four stood together staring at the structure. Kyle had taken out his ultrasound toy. Soon he was taking readings off the screen and was smiling at the team. The area outside of the block of the lotuses was six inches thick, but this block was only about an inch. It was hollow.

"It's the king's escape exit! Your gran was a genius, Akram!" Freddy cried in excitement.

Kyle bent down to try and break through and Akram held him back.

"Hold on, if we break through now, it will be a free access and some families out for a picnic may decide to explore. Wait, we'll come back tonight."

"Kyle, we will need a cover of NDMC to work here tonight."

NDMC was New Delhi Municipal Corporation. The India Gate area fell under NDMC and the team needed a cover when they worked at night in case some local police or bystanders stepped in out of curiosity.

"Consider it done, sir."

Freddy suddenly spoke up.

"Another important thing you folks are missing is the 'Pyramid Syndrome'."

Akram realised how valuable Freddy was to the team. He was dead right and everyone had forgotten about this key aspect.

Kyle looked up and asked, "Pyramid? I thought we are going under... not climbing up...What do you mean, sir?"

Akram was nodding at Freddy.

"Freddy is damn right. In Egypt, it was realised that anyone who entered a new discovery of a pyramid or a Tomb, was at risk of breathing in air that was almost hundreds of years old. Sometimes, stale air had particulate matter that would get inhaled, causing severe lung infection and sometimes even death. Historians sometimes attributed this to a curse, but science soon discovered what was happening. We will need masks that can help filter the air. Kyle, we can use the Sarin gas masks we had procured for the North Korean project."

Everyone nodded in agreement and Freddy was beaming with delight at the value add he was proving out to be for the team.

Akram also realised there was one more piece of equipment they needed.

"Kyle, also get the high frequency detonator for quick entry."

The high frequency detonator was a new technology developed by the Dutch. It involved drilling small holes in any wall, stone, rock that was an obstruction, filling it with a special gel and then applying a high frequency vibrating unit to the obstruction. In a matter of a minute, the obstruction would crumble without any blasts or other noise.

"Sir, already procured." Akram nodded and then addressed everyone.

"Okay folks, we are off now and we will be back at 1 a.m. I suggest we all get back and get a couple of hours of rest."

* * *

As Freddy sat in the car with the team, he felt a sense of achievement. From the feelings of betraying his country, he was now convinced that this had to be done. This was not the death of a patriot, but a reminder of what the country truly stood for. He could not but feel enormous pride at what Indians managed in the early 1900s. A bloody tunnel! He smiled. "Aha, now I know where Akram gets his wits from. Brilliance runs in his veins."

CHAPTER 18
THE ASSAULT ON THE VICEROY HOUSE

New Delhi
2015

A hundred years later than when it was planned to be used, the King's escape would prove to be the ingress route for the RAW unit. It was, perhaps, ironical that the task set upon by a group of freedom fighters would be used that night by another set of patriots. On their return to the safehouse, Akram had briefed Freddy about the location of the guest house that was to house their Chinese guest. It was a location in Gurgaon. Freddy was now to take charge of the location and prep it, for the Chinese delegate. Already, Kyle had deputed two assets who were fluent in Mandarin. Akram had used his UAE based 'Export house' to rent the house in the last forty-eight hours. Documents move fast when you offer fifty percent higher value than the market.

A heated debate had broken out when they returned, whether Akram and Samdup be allowed to tag along with the teams. Kyle was very clear that once the teams left the guesthouse, he was in charge and he would not allow Samdup or Akram to tag along at all.

"You are putting the team at risk. It has been twelve years since you went on any 'picnic' sir."

'Picnic' was a team nickname for operations. Picnic by the sea or picnic up the hills were self explanatory descriptors of the terrain of the operation. Akram was out of physical shape, given his knee injuries in his last operation and two months full of steroids had destroyed his body's immunity. Samdup was in much better shape, but he agreed with Kyle that they should not even think of going along.

"Come on Akki, let's not get all emotional here. You know it's a bullshit idea."

Finally, Akram had taken a call and announced to the team that it was an executive decision and he *would* go along, but as a 'follow the lead' guest, which meant that he would stay twenty metres behind the team and the team was given the instruction that no effort would be made to protect or rescue Akram, should he get 'compromised'.

Kyle threw up his hands in disgust. "So be it sir... I am catching a power nap. Wakey 01.18 a.m., ETD 3 a.m."

The teams were now in operation mode. Their food and sleep would follow a standard operations protocol. They had had only high-calorie dense foods such as dry fruits. Just preops, they would gulp down a high sugar caffeine drink specially engineered for such situations.

Akram tried to catch some sleep, but it was impossible. It just seemed unreal. The entire chain of events of the last eighteen hours were like a blur. On top of this, he had even uncovered a hundred-year old tunnel under the Rashtrapati Bhawan! He thought of his Didima and smiled. He so admired her. Of course, there was a long story she had told him about why the tunnel could never be used, but then that was a story for another day.

He called home and in a quick chat updated Aarti. Aarti had, in her custody a document with access codes to Akram's entire wealth. He had prepared a central location, a bank locker with all details that Aarti would need. Aarti listened to Akram. She never expected that Akki would go for another picnic now, after so many years. She paused and then reacted.

"This is quite a tale, eh! Anjali would love to hear it from you, Akki. Do what you have to. This came with the job, didn't it? Get it over with. I know you have thought this through and this is the correct path. Call me once you start for home, I'll get some khichdi made... good night!"

Akram smiled. Khichdi with yellow lentils had been his comfort food for years and Aarti knew it was a big stress buster for Akram. He was happy that Aarti too agreed with him. Before he knew it, Akram had fallen into a deep sleep. It was two hours to wakey time!

* * *

At 01.15 hrs, the team's watches buzzed.

The teams were prepped and ready for departure briefing at 02.15 a.m. The RAW protection team was executing a historical first – an assault on India's prime symbol of democracy, the Rashtrapati Bhawan. Such larger issues were hardly on top of anyone's mind. Akram was going around the teams making small talk and cracking jokes. It was a leadership trait.

Samdup spoke up.

"Team 02.35 a.m. We will gather for a briefing in two."

Norbu who was leading four units and Kyle who was leading the other four would lead two teams. Operations always had two units. Smaller teams with leaders were always swifter and able to take quick decisions. In two minutes, the full team was in the conference room. As a reminder, the screen still had the red dots blinking reminding everyone why they were doing what they were doing.

Akram was dressed in the regular 'picnic dress' – jet black body-hugging suits and specially designed Israeli shoes. As he stood in front of the team, he nodded at the team leaders.

"I have set up a new challenge for this team this time. We will not take any live munition. I though I could slip in blanks without you guys knowing it, but how can I ask you to blindly trust me if I do that."

As he spoke, he pulled out his 9 mm side arm and in full view slid the magazine out and one by one threw the bullets on the table in a dramatic flourish. He slid the magazine back, slid back the cocking channel and even threw out the one bullet in the chamber.

"I know Norbu and Kyle have already had you empty out your weapons. We will also not need arm to arm combat weapons that may injure or accidentally kill our fellow countrymen. You know that I will die before I injure a fellow Indian. The team in the Rashtrapati Bhawan are your fellows, trained by the best and they will still have the right to use weapons at you. Our task is to slip in, use our training to render the on-ground team weaponless, and capture our target and return in six minutes. We believe we know where the guest will be and if all goes well, we will be able to access him in 120 seconds from exit at the RB. Vikas and Arjun are medico leads and will take charge of the guest."

He nodded at the two, who nodded back. All were dressed in standard black with green and black camouflage face paint.

Medico training focused on battle wounds and also the ways to keep a subject drugged and yet responsive.

"I was also concerned about what happens after we come back. How will this operation be classified? Hence, I have issued formal communication from my official id of this operation. This protects you from any state action by the government as you are following orders.

"I must ask you once again that if anyone feels otherwise, they should simply walk away from this operation. Anyone?"

Akram looked around the room. His tone was honest and genuine. Not one eye flickered as all gazed at him.

"Okay folks, we are on. By the way, I am just tagging along at the back. Don't worry about me, I am only going to taste the cashewnut barfi they serve at the RB. It's delicious."

The team broke out in a laugh.

"We are off, Sammy. See you at the Gurgaon station."

Akram turned and hugged Samdup in a tight embrace and Samdup's eyes welled up. He would give his life for Akram and the last four days had only confirmed what Samdup always knew that Akram was a man to follow blindly.

Samdup had engaged with the 'art director' in RAW to help set up the stage at the fountain entrance. The art director in RAW was an incredible team. They would acquire the right props to set up the stage. In this case, they wanted to be sure that no local civilian or police interrupted them while they entered the ingress gate. And the gate had to be covered back. So the location has been cordoned off at 1 a.m. with vans with LPG gas. Wooden screens saying 'Repair in Progress' had already been set up. A fire tender had also been requisitioned and was kept to make it look real. A stage production team would be standing in to respond to any curious onlookers or local police, if they showed up.

The teams were now moving in two vans towards the location.

As the vans reached the location, they saw the area barricaded off. It looked so real. The vans slid along with one of the large screens and everyone disembarked silently behind the screen. The production team, unaware of what was happening were just following orders. They thought it was some kind of a drill.

At 01.55 hours, the teams were standing in two parallel lines. Norbu was the demolition expert. As he signalled, everyone whipped out their air filter masks and put them on. The masks had a large visor so the vision was not impaired.

Norbu used a small battery-operated drill machine and started drilling three two-inch holes to place a demolition charge.

The team faced the first surprise of the day when Norbu noticed that in just one inch, the drill gave way and he realised that the tile was just one inch deep. A demolition charge would not be required. He quickly used the drill at two more locations. He soon had slipped through three hooks through the holes. The hooks were like arrow heads, easy to get in but they would be difficult to pull out. In three minutes, the hooks were in place and Norbu handed one end to Kyle and one to Arjun. He looked at the team and hand signalled that they would all pull in five seconds.

In five seconds, Norbu's hand slashed down and all three pulled hard at the tile. The tile was about 5 feet by 4 feet. It broke into two pieces as it came out of the structure. There was a gush of air as the century old entrance was broken into. Akram was staring with focus and almost felt like an Egyptian tomb raider.

Kyle and Norbu looked at Akram and smiled. They were in.

Training took over and the teams took ingress positions. No one knew what they would encounter. Kyle barked a command into his visor

"Deploy MDU..."

The MDU were Miniature Drone Units. These were an amazing use case for drones. They were no larger than a wasp and were excellent reconnaissance tools. They had a range of 200 metres and could stay in the air for thirty minutes. They transmitted a live feed back to the team's visors. So, it was just not the controller who could see through the camera of the MDU, but the entire team.

In the next ten seconds, a single MDU was activated and gently let through the opening. Akram too could use his visor. The visor was always engineered on the right eye and could be pulled down or up, depending on when it was being used. Akram knew it was a historical event, seeing the first images of a century old king's escape.

The MDU had a powerful set of lights, including lasers. The team could now see the images. It was an amazing sight. The drone had already done a 360 degree scan of the immediate area post the entrance. It had followed the tunnel that showed steps going down about twenty feet. Post the descent, the drone mapped the ten feet high tunnel that was almost eighteen feet in width. Incredibly, they could see vegetation inside.

Kyle remarked.

"Vegetation? That's amazing. This means there is ventilation and the air is breathable. Anyway, let's keep our masks on to be careful. How on earth did anyone plan ventilation. All the way to RB?"

Akram saw the visuals and remarked.

"The designer, crafty as he was, has used the water bodies. See how the tunnel is headed right under the water bodies. The corners are being used for ventilation."

The MDU had moved forward and they could see cobbled floors, obviously designed to provide a stable floor for horses to gallop through. Horses found smooth surfaces very difficult to run on and hence all roads were always designed in a way so that the surface was never smooth.

Almost two minutes had passed.

Kyle snapped, "Go... Go... Go..."

In unison, the teams hunched down to take positions and started entering the tunnel one by one. Thanks to the drone, they knew exactly what was ahead. The LED flashlights on the visors gave a good spread of light to let them see ahead. The teams went down the stairs. Akram followed the two teams, but could not help notice the design elements on the ceiling and the cornice. He smiled to himself. A tunnel with carvings. Someone must truly love their job to think of these designs in an escape tunnel.

The teams had now reached the bottom of the staircase and the visor lights from the nine members had lit up the tunnel. There were vine creepers and foliage on the bottom.

Kyle snapped, "Move swiftly."

The teams moved to the edges, one to each side of the tunnel and soon started moving forward. Akram was trying his best to keep pace. He was out of breath already and he was wondering if his decision of coming along had been a correct one.

Soon, everyone's visors saw a red flash on the visor screens and a warning beep in their earpieces. The MDU was flashing a warning. Its apparatus had identified an object ahead, but it was not easy to identify.

"Hold!" Kyle held his hand in the air. The MDU controller put some speed into the drone and it soon hovered around the object it had identified. The object was about fifty metres ahead. Soon, they could see it on their visors. It was an incredible video of a long rack of what appeared to be swords, helmets and weapons of several kinds. There was also an amazing rack of, what were very clearly, rifles and two large containers ahead. The drone did a scan and as nothing else was found, the controller turned the warning off.

"Move swiftly!"

Soon, the teams were sprinting ahead and reached the spot where the drone was still stable in the air.

Akram too reached the spot and was seeing the cache of arms that were present

Norbu held up a rifle, "What are these swords doing here? And rifles? The rifles are 1905 Springfields. Wow, never held one of them!"

Akram spoke in an excited tone, "Remember, this is a king's escape. Imagine, if you are escaping from the RB and you are facing some form of aggression, this is the best place to arm yourself before you exit the tunnel. Amazing how well thought through this is, isn't it?"

Norbu had opened the two boxes. "Ammunition for the rifles and good lord, some sticks of explosives!"

The teams had been given a background and they were all amused to find their encounter with history. By a stroke of luck the very premise of a kings's escape had helped the freedom fighters build a tunnel where the unsuspecting British had provided even the weapons at what they thought was the exit, but was actually the entry point.

Norbu had to get the attention back to the project.

"We move now, teams."

The visor lights pierced ahead.

"MDU scan," Kyle snapped

The controller had taken custody of the unit to save battery. The MDU hovered and then leapt forward. Soon the streaming video from fifty metres ahead showed an empty tunnel. The air was getting heavier and dusty.

Akram remarked to the teams as he tried to keep up.

"Looks like the space under the water bodies has ended. So poor ventilation ahead... see how the height has gone up."

Norbu looked up and noticed that the height had increased.

"Yes, we can move faster now, it's 0325. I will ask production team to close shop and prepare for the 5 a.m. stage set up."

With this, Norbu relayed his commands to the production unit at the entrance. The team would clean out the space, replace the broken part under the fountain and then leave a four-member team in civvies to ensure no one noticed anything wrong or tried to access the entrance.

It has been quite simple so far. Soon, the teams noticed that the tunnel sloped upwards.

"We are climbing up Raisina Hill. We're close –another 180 metres," Kyle noted.

The teams were moving at a fast pace now. The MDU kept at a fifty-metre ahead space, streaming video to the team. The cobbled floors were just so easy to get a good grip on. The teams noticed that every fifty metres, they would find small structures shaped like benches. "Resting spots for the escaping viceroy and his officers and family. They would assume there would be aged as well as children, so the tunnel design even took care of resting places."

Akram had noted the structures and remarked to the team. Kyle noticed the clear pride in Akram's voice now. He was wondering if they would ever sit around and discuss this picnic.

Kyle was the first to notice something in the video stream and he raised his hand. With this signal, both the teams abruptly stopped.

Norbu remarked, "Send MDU ahead another twenty metres please."

As the MDU sprang forward, they could see the structure come into shape and it turned out to be large steps going up.

Kyle motioned for everyone to move forward.

Soon, the two teams came to a large structure with steps going up.

Kyle checked his GPS and noted,

"Okay, we're just under our exit point. Let's take a breather."

Soon Akram had also caught up with the teams.

Norbu nodded to the medics and remarked, "Please check evac equipment, boys. We don't know if subject will be able to walk or be cooperative, so eighty percent probability is that you have to knock him out for forty-five minutes and carry him out."

The medic team noted and soon were accessing the carry-on equipment they were carrying. Included in the same was a foldable stretcher. "Okay to go..." the medic team noted to Kyle.

Akram came to the base of the steps.

"Get the MDU scan done please... let's see where this goes. Once we have the lay of the land, we have time to kill, boys. Our info tells us that dinner is to be served at 7.18 p.m. sharp. This structure was built in 1921, has 340 rooms and 200,000 sq feet area. So, it is important that our information is accurate. Trying to comb this structure for our guest will be an impossible task. Norbu has planned this snatch, and it should be a three-four minute operation. We don't know what is the structure at the exit, whether it is stone or a simple tile like the entrance. So, we will figure that out in the next two hours or so. As the 36 hours post the op will be high-energy, we will all catch up on sleep till 3 p.m. Clear?"

Both the teams barked, "Clear" in unison.

The controller sent the MDU up the staircase and the streaming video was coming onto the visors now. The tunnel had sloped down quite a bit and Norbu noticed that the stairs went up nearly eighteen feet. The MDU came against a dead wall and hovered waiting for a command.

"Dead end, forty steps in a circuitous route," the controller shared with the teams.

Norbu signalled to his demolition expert.

"Asif and I are going up to check the exit."

Akram responded immediately.

"Please take two more mates, Norbu. We don't know what's ahead and I don't want any surprises."

Kyle signalled to two of his team members, who sprang forward.

Akram also signalled to the controller, "Keep MDU on Exit till they come back. I want full visual while they are there."

Norbu and three men soon began going up the stairs. They noticed that the sides of the stairs even had an in-built grip to help the infirm come down the stairs.

Soon the four reached the dead-end wall and the team had their ultrasound device out to measure the thickness and material of the structure.

As the machine hummed and scanned, Norbu looked at the structure, it was 8 feet in height and 4 feet in width. Like a good door should be, he thought.

"It's a special type of mortar and concrete structure, but the reader is showing a 6-inch thickness. That is crazy. Six inches of thickness? There are no hinges as well. How does the damn thing open. If I use my vibration mode, there will be a loud noise audible for 100 feet around the door."

"What? Six inches! We need to break through six inches, team!"

Akram was watching on the visor and remarked.

"Hmmm, that is quite strange. We need to think guys. Whoever planned this had to design an entrance on the other side that was easy to use. You think the viceroy's family with maybe small children would be equipped to blast this open? No, it can't be! We need to think of something. Did you notice the entrance door... how simple that was. Something isn't right."

"Maybe the door is on hinges from the other side. Maybe there's a lever on the other side. Use the lever and the door opens," Vinod the medic spoke up.

Akram was quick to react, "And why don't you just slip through the damn wall of concrete and push the bloody lever from the other side?" He was livid at the ridiculous suggestion being made.

Kyle was quick to jump to his defence.

"I think what Vinod means is that if there is a lever to move the door, then we have to find some linkage to the door from this side. Such a heavy piece and we can't even see any frame of a door. Not even a speck of a crack."

Akram noticed the quick reaction by Kyle to defend his team mate. He always appreciated leaders who didn't just join the boss in making fun of team mates.

"Oh! I see, Vinod that's a thought then. How do we figure this out then?"

Akram was stumped. The designer in this case knew that the freedom fighters would access the door from this side. It can't be that someone forgot to put in the most important thing for the entire operation – a way to enter the Viceroy House from the other side of the door!

Blasting the door was an impossible idea. That would send alarm bells all around. Akram knew that the RB was even quipped with a seismic gauge. This helped detect any vibrations to prevent anyone trying to break through the floor or the lawns. In fact, he was aware that while the RAW was not involved, special operations in the armed forces had undertaken a three-month operation to imagine all possible ways to enter the RB. The ground had been the most sensitive and hence the seismic readers had been installed at several locations.

His focus came back to the scene on his visor. What could they be missing?

"Patch me to Sammy, K."

Kyle used the router installed by the team at the entrance and connected Akram to Sammy.

"Yes Akki, I can see you guys on the visual feed. Am wondering about the door myself."

"Sammy, recall that op in Turkey where we had to get that vault door open using cutters—"

Samdup cut Akram mid-sentence.

"No Akki, that won't work. This is far heavier."

"Sammy, check the map. Can there be another exit? Another route that we have missed?"

"Wait, rolling out the canvas as we speak... Hmmm... wait... I can't locate the route. It's too detailed, damnit!"

Akram was getting impatient. "Sammy, just follow the line of the tunnel."

"Yes, the line of the tunnel. You mean the line of the miniature lotuses. Yes, here it is... and... no. Just one line, Akki. No other route. In fact, no lotuses even close by."

"No lotuses close by?"

Samdup suddenly shrieked.

"The damn lotus. Akki, how can you miss it? Every important location is marked by your grandpa's signature lotus, even the entrance had the lotus. Find the bloody lotus on the door!"

Akram leaped onto the staircase and bounded up the stairs. His team was taken aback.

He could only run up ten stairs before his bad knee caught up. He panted and started climbing slowly.

"Light up the door. I want it flooded. Find the symbol of a lotus."

Kyle had stayed on at the base and he signalled for the battery-operated LED flood lamps to follow Akram.

"On its way, sir."

By the time Akram reached the twenty-fifth stair, his team mate had already caught up with him.

"Go ahead. Go ahead. Run up and set it up."

As Akram reached the top, he was panting for breath. The door had been lit up with two miniature flood lamps. The team was going over the door inch by inch. After twenty minutes, not a single lotus symbol had been found on the door.

"So, nothing huh? No sign of a bloody lotus? Can it be that maybe they could not complete the full structure? Maybe they couldn't even make the door movement mechanism?"

Norbu was staring at the door.

"Why are we only looking at the door? Such a heavy door isn't just going to move on some hinges. We are looking at the door in a wrong way. There has to be a clue in the design."

Norbu speed dialled Samdup, "Sir, can you message me a picture of the starting point of the tunnel?"

Soon Sammy had sent a picture of the canvas to Norbu. Norbu enlarged the picture. Akram peered over the screen and saw the row of lotuses starting from the middle of the Viceroy House.

Akram could not make any other trail of lotuses.

“Nothing at all.”

“Wait, sir, am I wrong or is this very first lotus inverted 180 degrees?”

Akram leapt back to the screen and enlarged the screen further.

“Bloody hell, you are right, but that could just be a mistake, right? No... no, this architect is a perfectionist. No way. This is done purposefully. What does this mean? Is it a message?”

Norbu said it aloud for his other team mates.

“A long row of lotus flower symbols but the starting symbol is inverted. What can that mean?”

Before Akram could react, Norbu had suddenly grabbed his hand and whispered.

“The designer is telling us to look the other way, opposite...”

“Opposite the door... goddamnit. There is something opposite the door.”

The team turned around and the floodlights were turned around to the opposite wall.

A collective gasp went around as all of them saw an engraved lotus right in the centre of the wall. It was about four inches by four inches.

“Another lotus,” remarked a team mate. “Did this architect also design the RB? I came to visit Mughal Gardens as a school kid and I remember that even the fountains inside the RB were designed in lotus formation.”

Akram smiled and thought to himself. The damn lotus is leading the way. His great grandfather even made the RB fountains in lotus shape.

Soon, Norbu had taken out his ultrasound scanner and he was taking readings from the lotus.

"The wall is concrete, but the area, six inches by six inches around the lotus is hollow. One inch thick only. Just like the entrance at the fountain. Should we break into it?"

Saying this, Norbu had nodded to his team mate who had reached out and taken a small hammer.

Akram gestured to him to stop.

"No... no... don't touch it. Will it trigger some mechanism to move the door? We aren't ready yet. It's too early. Take a picture and send the ultrasound readings to Sammy and patch me through."

Norbu had soon connected Sammy.

"So Sam, what say? How do you think this will go? Should we try to move this tile?"

"Akki, I think it best to be safe. What if it does trigger some movement in the door? We may be detected and our guest hasn't even landed in India. Let's wait for when we are ready and six minutes prior, we can try our best. I am guessing with the purpose in mind, I think the door movement will be rather swift. Clearly, the purpose to assassinate the viceroy would require that the door moves quickly. Let's have faith in his design process and leave it for when we are ready."

"Agreed. Ciao buddy."

Akram gestured to Norbu that they should all move down as there was not enough space for the entire team on the porch of the door. They might as well move down and plan scenarios and grab some rest.

The team moved down to the base. It was now a matter of waiting. Espionage players understand the importance of this critical period before a 'picnic'. Waiting for action and what one does in this period truly impacts an asset's performance in an operation. Some folks tend to take it so easy that they sleep through and it is only just before the operation that they try to break off the lethargy and it is too late. Some stay so stressed that they tire mentally and their alertness levels take a beating, leading to rash decisions. A balance between these two approaches is very critical.

Norbu and Kyle had already seen at least twelve operations in the field and were well trained. The time was 0530 p.m. The teams decided to take turns to rest and discuss scenarios. Each team would take an alternate one hour power nap. Freddy had already shared an event plan for the night. Akram knew a minute by minute agenda as well as location of the reception, dinner and discussion room. It was agreed to be Ops ready at 7 p.m. They would attempt to open the gate at 2005 hrs. the agenda stated that the guest would finish dinner at 2015 hrs and move to the discussion room, which was a six-seater meeting room close to the private dining hall. The RB had eight dining rooms, depending on the size of the gathering.

Norbu had identified that the catch would take place in the discussion room. They anticipated that as discussions may be confidential, the presence of security may be reduced. In any case, once inside the RB, only a small number of personal security would be allowed. They were unsure of which room the door would open into and what route would be needed to reach the discussion room. In the whole team, only Akram and one team member Adhiraaj had set foot inside the RB. Adhiraaj had been posted as part of the RB guards a few years back, and that was very useful. He had some idea of the lay of the structure and was confident that once he oriented himself after getting inside, he would be able to get some idea of the route to the discussion room.

This small group of Indians were now hours away from gatecrashing a party in the "Viceroy House".

CHAPTER 19
CHAOS AND CONFRONTATION

New Delhi
2015

At 1900 hours, the two teams were up and about. Final shots of energy drinks and protein bars were consumed along with high sugar bars to boost up energy available for the body, especially for the brain. Akram, too, consumed the same diet. At 1950 hrs, Akram and Norbu had climbed up the staircase and were carefully scraping the area around the symbol. Only the symbol was hollow. It would have taken some work to carve out a hole in the middle of a solid rock face.

Akram remarked.

"Look, I believe the hollow plate will trigger some mechanism to move the door. It is clear that the door needs to move swiftly and without needing too much strength. I am wondering if it can be some kind of high strength swivel hinge? What if the door gets stuck midway? After all, we are trying this after almost 100 years, eh?"

Norbu responded to Akram in a grave voice, "Sir, with all due respect, we will never know what the designer thought of, will we? We only know he was ultra smart and had geared the entire tunnel for access through the fountains. So I am sure, provided the mechanism has not got spoilt, that the door will indeed move swiftly. Failing which we have no option but to just blast our way through. Okay?"

Akram stared at Norbu and rolled up his eyes

"Blast the door... Good lord. I shudder at the thought. Hold on. What is that?"

Akram had looked up at the ceiling as he reacted to Norbu's idea of blasting the door, and as he looked up, he saw something shine.

He grabbed a floodlight and threw the light onto the ceiling. From the porch, the ceiling was at least twelve feet. Right on top, Norbu and Akram saw a large block of stone in a metal cage. It was at least 5 feet by 8 feet in width. The metal cage seemed sturdy and surprisingly had not caught rust. How could that be? Norbu let out a whistle and called out to the MDU controller.

"Send up our baby asap to the ceiling. Can you see through by visor?"

The team below could see the structure, and the controller quickly sent the drone to inspect it.

Soon, they all could see close-ups of the structure. The large rock face was sitting inside the cage, and it was clear that if the cage broke, this boulder would come crashing down.

"So gentlemen, what are we looking at?" Akram asked the team.

Kyle responded immediately.

"It's some kind of weapon. I think to prevent anyone from following the escaping family. See how it is located just after the door. I think the security detail of the royal family would use that to just knock off anyone pursuing them."

"Anyone else?"

There was silence.

"Well, as I see it..." Akram remarked, "We just don't know. So let's leave it at this. All I know is boys, when we break the tile, we may trigger something so just keep the hell away from the area under that rock!"

Kyle remarked.

"Sir, it's 1945 hrs. Action time, team!"

Soon, the two teams had aligned themselves in two rows next to the door, helmets down, to prevent any bomb fragments injuring them.

Akram had suggested that he'd break the plate as it seemed quite thin.

At 1950 hrs, Akram Khan, the great grandson of India's first member of the Royal Architecture society took a small hammer and broke a 100 year old seal. Every one was awestruck as the hammer hit the seal. The seal broke easily. Akram had used just enough force so as not to trigger something inside the chamber. As the pieces crumbled to the ground, Akram could see nothing.

"What the hell?"

He then snatched a flashlight from his belt and shone it inside the cavity.

Lit by a powerful LED flashlight, the chamber inside was empty, except for a small piece of string that Akram could see. The string was shining and appeared to be metallic. His fingers reached inside to grab it.

"Alright boys, there is some string which appears metallic. I am going to pull it so let's be ready... *Now!*"

Akram pulled the string, but nothing happened. As he pulled the string-like wire outside, it just slipped out of the chamber.

"Looks like it's long piece." Akram pulled on the string and it started giving way and coming out of the the cavity slowly. Akram noticed that as the string fell to the ground, it started to become thicker and thicker. Akram noticed the string turn to a thin rope and then in a minute, the rope had become quite a thick piece. In another few seconds, he was holding onto a thick rope.

And then, Akram could feel he could not easily pull the rope. It had become taut.

"Okay, so it's not pulling anymore. I am about to pull with some force, so please stand by, team."

Akram wrapped the rope around his arm, softly pulled till the rope was taut and then slowly increased the pressure. He kept slowly increasing the pressure, but nothing happened.

"It's not working. Damn it!"

He tried doing the exercise again, but nothing happened.

Norbu saw the disappointment in Akram's eyes.

"Sir, please allow me. I believe there must be some concealed system that will help move the door. It must have got stuck with the passage of time. May I give it a try?"

Akram noticed Norbu's body shape and his bulging biceps and thought it was a good idea to use some old-fashioned muscle power.

He stepped aside and slowly unwrapped the rope, handing it over to Norbu.

Norbu wrapped the rope till it became taut. Then contrary to Akram's process of slowly increasing pressure, he let go of the rope till it was almost free. Then taking a wide step stance, he grabbed the rope with both his hands and gave a strong, sudden jerk. The rope suddenly gave way and Norbu fell back onto his team mates.

"Bloody hell, it tore!" Akram screamed in anger. But before he could utter another word, the entire team heard a creaking sound from behind the door and they could hear moving parts and suddenly there was a loud sound from the ceiling. As the lamps were already trained on the boulder on the top, they all turned up to look at the source of the sound.

Awestruck, they saw the metal cage move on its own and suddenly, without a warning, the base of the cage swung open as the mammoth rock face began to fall down.

Akram screamed, "*Watch out, it's falling!*"

And then, as if by magic, the boulder instead of falling to the ground, started moving down in a slow motion. Norbu whispered sharply in the background:

"The door... the door... it's friggin' moving."

Almost in slow motion, the teams saw the wonder of a pulley system made a hundred years back. The large boulder on the top was made to the perfect weight which was a little heavier than the door weight. Hence as the metal cage gave way, gravity came into play and the heavier rock fell slowly to the ground, pulling the main door up. It was almost like magic seeing the door rise up into some cavity on the top.

"*Ya allah!* Will you look at this? Almost without a sound even after hundred bloody years! They have used gravity... gravity to do this."

Kyle snapped.

"Team, action ready!"

As the door rose up, they saw a wall ahead.

"Another wall? What the hell!" said Akram.

"Calm down, sir, it wouldn't have been a door on the other side." Norbu put his hand on the wall.

"It's wood. It must be a façade on the wall. Cut away, please."

A team mate stepped forward, and using a high intensity laser, soon cut away a large block to allow them easy entry.

Norbu used the laser to also burn a small hole in the middle, inserted an arrowhead hook and soon pulled hard at the block. Even while the team had weapons without ammunition, they trained weapons at the door. As the wooden piece fell, Kyle peered into what seemed like a room without any lights.

He slowly edged into the room and after doing a quick scan, whispered,

"Empty room... looks like pantry storage."

He gestured an all clear and the entire team slipped inside the room.

Akram said a silent prayer. The team was inside one of the most protected buildings in the world.

There were cartons and cartons of food items and there was a metal door which looked like a large freezer room.

"It's the kitchen pantry storage," Adhiraaj whispered to the team. "It would be adjoining the west-wing kitchen."

The one key change that the team had done was to change into RB butler service uniforms. The dark grey shirts with black trousers and sleeveless Nehru jackets were the standard issue uniform inside the RB. Norbu had suggested this change to Akram. His view was that as they had no offensive arms to neutralise the staff inside the RB, they needed to blend in at least, so they could come close to use their Tibetan martial arts training to use nerve blocks to temporarily disable the staff. Akram thought it was a brilliant idea.

The RB uniformed 'service' team inside the pantry had asked Adhiraaj to start work with the MDU controller. They would fly out the smallest version of the drones that only had a battery life of twelve minutes and had a very basic camera to stream video back. It also made a low decibel noise that could be missed unless someone was very close to the drone. As Adhitraj had walked these corridors, he had to get familiar and guide the team.

Sitting next to the controller, they had made a station on a small table. The controller walked up to the entrance door which everyone noticed was a swivel door without any means for locking. He edged the door open and let the 'fly' out.

In the next six minutes, guided by Adhiraaj, they had made copies of a rough hand-drawn map of where they were. Akram noticed that the door was cleverly placed from an architecture design point of view as the main bedroom and six guest rooms had doors opening into a disbursal area right in front of the pantry door. Not commonly known was the fact that the pantry was actually part of the master bedroom till 1965 when the then-President found the room too ostentatious and had the pantry and one more bedroom carved out of the main bedroom.

The team now studied the map. The discussion room was a three-minute walk through long corridors. Adhiraaj knew that this area would have at least two perimeter security personnel doing a beat security round. The good news was that no one expected that a team would gain entry through a tunnel to a central area of the RB.

Akram studied the map and remarked,

"We will split into two teams. One team will lead and neutralise security detail. For god's sake I want minimum force. Remember these are our teams. So no broken bones please. Use the jugular block to knock them unconscious. The advance team will allocate one man to carry the security personnel back and we will keep them in the pantry well gagged and bound. The advance team therefore will make the path clear for the snatch team. Norbu will lead the snatch, so Kyle, you need to be the advance team."

Kyle and Norbu reacted with a quick, "Clear!" and nodded to Akram.

Akram also added that he would follow the snatch team.

"One more thing, remember you are RB service members so *do* not take crouch positions. Walk in pairs as if you are trainees being taken on a tour. Smile and chat. The first pair will stay at least twenty metres ahead of the team to spot RB staff and neutralise."

The teams got into formation. Adhiraaj was kept in the snatch team, just in case they lost their way around the two lakh sq feet compound. The pair in the front opened the door and the team stepped onto the thick carpet and started following the map now committed to memory. After a pause of twenty seconds, the other team walked out as well.

The first encounter happened in the next eighteen seconds itself. The advance pair had reached a right turn in the corridor and as they turned, they immediately spotted a pair of RB guards stationed near the very large French windows. As anticipated, seeing the uniforms and a pair of smiling faces did not raise any alarms. The two guards looked at them and hardly reacted.

As the balance team members turned the corner, they saw that the action had already ended as the advance team was rushing back, carrying the two guards on their shoulders. They would stay unconscious for only eight to ten minutes and they had to get them to the pantry and get them securely gagged and bound.

It was incredible that more security was not visible. The advance team was to return and just cover the main corridor in front of the pantry and clear the access for the team when they returned carrying the guest. An important discussion had been the fate of the Prime Minister. The agenda gave some good news that the President may not join them for discussions post-dinner, after which the Prime Minister and his core team would have a close door session with the guest in the eight seater discussion room.

Samdup had the view that if anyone even thought of snatching the PM, it was a clear sign of mutiny and a certain death sentence. Anyhow, Akram had argued they did not benefit from the PM in custody.

Akram still wasn't sure how the Indian government would react. A Chinese government official being kidnapped was an acutely embarrassing situation and he was sure that the country may unleash a massive reward for any information about the guest and the snatch team. He had decided he would worry about that later.

His mind returned as the team moved slowly through the corridor. It was agreed that unless it was an RB guard team, they would not react to any local service guys, unless someone asked any questions about the identity. They did cross a few junior bearers, but no one seemed to notice.

The team came across the second RB security pair just near the hallway from where the entrance to the discussion room was marked on the maps. Once again, the security personnel allowed the team too close, and before they could react, they had been immobilised. As they were quite some distance away from the pantry, they were bound and gagged and placed inside the nearest room in the hallway, which happened to be a reading room. There was a closet for cleaning items and the pair of RB guards were 'dropped' in the closet.

Luck, they say, favours the brave and uncannily the advanced team had now peeled off to monitor the corridor exiting from the hallway, while the four-member snatch team and Akram walked nonchalantly towards the discussion room. It was 2012 hrs. Akram noticed that the discussion room had a small tea serving area just outside the main room. They could see two RB service staff members setting up the equipment.

They quizzically looked up at the group that entered. Akram was quick to remark to put them at ease.

"Trainee batch support," Akram mentioned with a straight face.

"Oh, but why here? Only three guests. What will we do with so many? Please vacate this place. Who sent you? Was it Dilip?"

The team had come close to the two and at a simple nod from Akram, the two were soon overpowered. Bundling them into an adjacent room. Akram asked Adhiraaj and Atul to man the tea station. Akram and the other two-unit members entered the adjacent room which was a pantry storage area.

The two guys were gagged and bound. All they had to do was wait.

The team members outside were quickly familiarising themselves with the coffee machine. It would be quite suspicious if they were asked for coffee and all they could do was try to switch the machine on. It was 2018 hrs and appeared that the meeting was delayed. Akram and the team sat inside the adjacent room. The two RB service staff were struggling against the tightly-bound wrists and face gags. One of them was trying to grunt something.

Akram leaned forward and read his name tag that read 'Munir Ali'.

"Munir bhai, *hum aapke dost hai.* If I open your gag, if you shout, I will have to kill you. Do you understand?"

Munir violently nodded. Akram opened his gag. Munir coughed and wheezed.

"I am sorry... I won't shout. I am asthmatic and stress brings on an attack. Please give me my inhaler. Please, who are you? Please don't kill me, I have an old mother. Please... please!"

He was traumatised by the capture and the gag was making it worse.

"No problem, son. Where is your inhaler? Don't worry, we are here to meet your guests. As long as you cooperate, nothing is going to happen to you, okay?"

Munir nodded, tears streaming down his eyes. "It's in the right pocket of my trousers." He rolled over so Akram could access it. He took out the inhaler. He had experience with inhalers as his wife too used them occasionally.

"Okay, here you go. Let's do three quick puffs. One by one, okay.Not together."

In seconds, Munir's breathing had become steady and he too was calming down

"Thank you. Thank you."

Akram put the gag back on his mouth and glaring at both of them muttered.

"Just keep still and keep quiet. In ten minutes, you will be back at your job. Give us trouble and *Allah kasam,* your severed heads will be sent to your family by morning. Get me?"

Munir and his colleague nodded in fear.

"Guests arriving." Akram looked up and the team tensed up for action. They were minutes away from confronting the team that had conspired to capture eighteen of their mates. Now action was expected and there was no reason for pretence. All five had now pulled down their balaclava masks. Originating in a small town in Ukraine by the same name, balaclavas were the go-to masks for special operations.

"Guests inside discussion room," the spotter on the door whispered. "Service area is secure. No security personnel outside. No one has asked for any refreshments yet. Maybe we can have a coffee."

Akram stood up from his crouching position.

"Okay, gentlemen, let's meet our guests." Saying that, he grabbed the door and pulled it wide open.

CHAPTER 20
CHINESE WHISPERS

New Delhi
2015

As kids, one often played the game called Chinese Whispers. Children sat in a circle or a straight line. The host gave a word or a string of words to the child at one end and each child whispered the expression to the child next to him. By the time the last child heard the expression, it turned out to be very different than the original expression. It was quite a racist expression and at least in South Asia, it was a norm not to use such expressions.

No one realised that they would soon be a witness to the same game in the hallowed halls of the erstwhile Viceroy House.

Akram and his four colleagues now stepped out of the adjacent room into the service area. Akram gestured to one of the units behind the coffee machine to take a guard position outside the service room to alarm the team and ward off any intrusion as much as possible. The fact that no security detail was inside was a comforting thought. The threat perception deep inside the RB was very low, and rightfully so.

The second unit member who was managing the coffee machine was gesticulating to Akram. Akram moved closer to him.

"Sir, there are loud arguments, almost a verbal spat happening. Three subjects. PM sir, Chinese guest and another Indian."

As Akram came closer to the door, he could also hear loud voices and someone almost shouting. The discussion rooms were sound protected so the only sound that was coming out was from the door. Akram also realised that as the guest had studied in India, he probably spoke English and even understood Hindi. Could the third guest be an interpreter?

Akram stepped closer to the door, turned the round knob and opened the door just a crack to better hear the discussion. Immediately, Akram could make out that the third Indian was the CDC, General Deshpande. Swamy Sir had always warned him to be wary of Deshpande. So the CDC was part of the meeting. What is the story he is cooking here now, Akram wondered.

He could now hear Liu Rongji speaking in a very loud voice. He signalled to his team to step back into the pantry area. He took off his balaclava so that just in case someone did walk into the room, they would just see two RB service staff. The remaining four members walked back surprised at this turn of events.

Akram stood right next to the door and listened to the conversation.

"General, it was a promise. He needs to go back with me. You cannot now do this. This is blackmail. PM sir, you heard the President. I am a loyal friend to India. Please stop this now. This is not right. You are playing me."

Liu was almost begging. Akram was mystified.

General Deshpande was now responding

"Your Excellency, this is also not fair. At the outset we had submitted our request. We need physical presence of our assets here in India. We cannot proceed. PM sir, I request you not to please give into Mr Rongji's request. We will not release him like this."

"General Deshpande, you idiot! How dare you change our terms now? You have misled your government. You are a liar. You Indians always do this. Keep bargaining and bargaining. You know what will happen if I make a single phone call to Beijing?"

Akram heard the PM speak.

"Mr Rongji, please calm down. Let's not fight like children. Just like your child, I too need to protect my children, right?"

Akram was just not able to understand what the hell was happening here. Rongji's 'child' was in Indian custody?

"No PM sir, you calm down. I want custody *now.* I have tried my best to help you for the last whole month and I am here to take Caihong. Do you know the risk I have taken to help you? You would have seen a blood bath, I tell you. *You are so ungrateful!*" Liu Rongji was now shouting.

"I demand you produce him now. Mr PM sir. *Now or I call home now... now... now!*"

There was an eerie silence.

Then Akram heard the PM Shri Narottam Singh speak up in a firm but reasonably stern tone.

"Mr Liu Rongji, stop this tantrum. I am also tired of playing with soft gloves on this issue. General sahib has been warning me to deal with a firmer hand, but all throughout, I have been patient with you and have gone out of our way to help your son, Mr Rongji. You do know selling hard drugs of over ten kg quantity to young children in India is such a heinous crime that your son will serve at least eighteen years in an Indian prison.

I believe you have to appreciate that we are here to help you. Please do not, again, raise your voice with me or threaten me. To top it, your son was seeking the Dalai Lama's travel plans to assassinate him. It's preposterous! We appreciate your help so far, but to go forward, you have to heed to General sahib. The sheer confidentiality is the reason that we are having this meeting. No record will be kept or minutes taken for obvious reasons. We understand you have been very helpful to us, but please also understand our view. This is our humble appeal."

Akram was bewildered. So India was blackmailing a senior Chinese government representative? For what? The trade deal? He could not help but admire the PM's hard and soft approach. It was a perfect route to keep a balance with a foe.

General Deshpande spoke up in a very calm tone.

"Mr Rongji, what you have done is indeed very brave, to allow us access to the information you have so far provided. We will always be in your debt and please be rest assured that we take care of our friends. Your son is under house arrest in a safe location in Kangra district just near the Gaggal airport. There's a direct two hour flight to Delhi. All you have to do is give us the location and safe passage for our eighteen member team and your son will be on a flight."

Akram could now hear the Chinese guest speak up. He was speaking in a low tone and Akram could make out that he was sobbing. What in heaven's name was going on? Where was the trade deal discussion? What eighteen did the General mean?

"General Deshpande! *Aap samajh nahin rahen hai! Main bahut trouble mein hu,*" he spoke in good Hindi with a Chinese accent. "You just don't understand, do you? How can I let you know the locations? My party will know, and the ones who don't like you very much! My family will be butchered. *You just don't understand, you bloody Indian!"*

The next few seconds went in a blur. From the crack in the door, Akram could see Liu get up from his chair violently. In one move, he had bent down and extracted a thin blade from his shoe and was rushing towards Deshpande.

He was now shouting, *"Get my son here, you useless bastard!"*

Akram had opened the door slightly to see Liu rush towards the door. Akram had guessed that the CDC was sitting just in front of the door. Years of training took over. Akram yelled to his team, "Now!" and opened the door. He did not even realise that he had taken his balaclava off. His focus was now on protecting a fellow Indian from being attacked by a Chinese government official.

Akram yanked the door open, leaped inside and crashed into Liu, throwing him on the large mahogany table behind him. General Deshpande was frozen in shock. Had Liu reached the General, some blood would certainly have been spilled.

Akram disarmed Liu and held him in a tight neck grip with his one arm twisted behind him. Liu was in pain and was gasping for breath.

The four team members in RB staff uniform, but wearing their balaclavas, rushed in taking vantage positions near the windows, the door and behind the PM and General Deshpande.

PM Narottam Singh's mouth had dropped and his eyes were wide in disbelief. General Deshpande could hardly stand straight. He was still recovering from the sight of a crazed Chinese rushing towards him with a six-inch blade. To top that, the room had been ambushed by RB staff wearing balaclavas.

Was this a terrorist attack? Where was the security? How did they reach there?

For seconds, there was an eerie silence in the room. The first words came from the PM.

"Who are you? What is happening? Please release our guest right now." He stepped forward towards Akram, at which instance Adhiraaj stepped into his way, stopping him.

"I said release Mr Liu right now."

Akram realised that he was not wearing a balaclava. He released Liu after snatching the blade from his hand. Liu, of course, assumed this was security. He gave his weapon up and crashed onto the chair sobbing, "My son. Please release my son. I beg you. I beg you PM sir. I beg you."

Narottam Singh too sat down in his chair.

"Mr Liu, looks like we have an interesting night ahead of us. These men are not RB staff. Especially not with these masks."

He addressed Akram, "You... you are not wearing a mask. Are you part of RB service or with these terrorists? I demand an explanation."

Akram stared back at the PM and at the General.

"Mr Prime Minister, I think today we will be asking the questions. You three gentlemen in this room are up to some mysterious deal and I need to know everything. As far as you are concerned, Mr Liu. You will enjoy our hospitality now. So, Mr Prime Minister, could you tell us what's happening here? You folks certainly look guilty! In any case, Mr Liu is coming with us, so we can extract information from him as well."

"Guilty? Mind your tone, Mr Terrorist. Guilty of what? Do you think I am scared? You will not be able to take Mr Liu.

Do you know the level of security we have outside? I don't know how you managed to get in. I suggest you surrender, or your bodies will be carried out. Trust me. Our boys won't forgive you."

"Our boys, Mr PM... I am part of 'our boys'! You, sir, are guilty of sacrificing eighteen of my resources in China. You sold the country for a miserable trade deal. And eighteen Indians have disappeared. Mr Liu will be our exchange solution."

At Akram's response, Liu spoke up.

"Hahah. Funny. Another group of Indians breaking into RB for the same information. No one knows what's happening in India. What lousy security you have! So now, these guys also want your spies, and so do you. So who wants the location first? Come on boys! Let's toss a coin, eh!" he raised his voice at Akram.

"What do you think we are doing? The last two weeks you guys have made my life hell. Why are you so chaotic? Have you seen your roads, eh? Have you seen the chaos? Here, there, everywhere! Chaos outside and chaos inside... even inside the Rashtrapati Bhawan!" The guest was ranting now.

It was Akram's turn to be crestfallen and puzzled. What was going on here?

General Deshpande spoke as he moved close to Akram.

"You are Akram Khan, aren't you, son? Mr PM, meet Akram. Leader, Project Chexo and Swamy's right hand. He was the person I was telling you about."

Akram had met the general several times along with Swamy sir. He had a good memory to recall him.

The General continued, "I don't know Akram, what you are doing here along with, I presume, some of your unit members from RAW? Don't you know you are not authorised to launch operations on Indian soil? Can you please tell us what is happening here? How did you even get inside?"

Akram took a deep breath, "I am sorry, General. I don't have time to answer your questions. All I want are my eighteen team mates. And I want to ensure their safe return. All eighteen. I lose one and I will drop Mr Liu from a twentieth floor of a building."

CDC was not amused at Akram's tone.

"Mind your tone, son. I want you to stand down and step outside the room. I will call for security and you will be taken into custody for action to follow. Damnit, take off those damn balaclavas!"

Before Akram could respond, PM Narottam Singh had raised his hand.

"Wait, General sahib. We have here a marvellous example of our Indian genius. How did these boys even get in? Amazing. They carry no weapons, and in fact, I think you owe him a big 'thank you' as Mr Liu may have been somewhat harmful to you had Mr Khan not intervened."

He stepped to the other end of the room. He addressed Akram.

"Son, those 18 are more valuable to me than you can imagine. They are safe, unhurt and we will get them home. I won't rest till they come home!"

Akram was confident that his instincts were always right. He felt a calm peace in what he just heard. The fact that his 18 team members were safe sent waves of happiness down his spine. He almost lost his balance and took help of the central table to hold himself. They were safe. He knew it to be true in his heart. He had not lost them. He could live again. He sighed and looked at the Prime Minister

"Mr Prime Minister, I certainly pray that you are right."

However, it was evident that there was total confusion in the room. The very members of the establishment, who Akram thought had handed over his team members to the Chinese, were assuring him that they were headed home.

He looked at the PM with a quizzical expression and raised his eyebrows at the PM. "I am confused. First you break into my systems and steal the list, and now you are telling me you are getting them home? I think something is amiss. I do hope this is not some ruse."

The Prime Minister smiled at Akram.

"I think we owe them an explanation and information can flow freely from both sides. Akram, please have one of your boys safely seat Mr Liu outside and ply him with his favourite jasmine tea. Mr Liu, you mentioned chaos. You will see how we create marvel after marvel from this chaos. Kindly wait outside."

Akram signalled to his team and the member closest to Akram took Liu by his arm outside.

"Okay, Mr Akram Khan ..." the PM continued, "Let us begin, as they say, at the beginning. For a few months now, we have been keen to create a very strong partnership with China. I have a close personal rapport with the Chinese Premier. We agreed that we will work to create a trade deal that will be the envy of the world. We are the world's two most populous countries. We can be large markets for each other. If we worked closely together, we could capture eighty percent of the world's manufacturing. If we controlled our prices, we could make good margins and help raise millions out of poverty. Today the developed world plays one against the other. If we got together, it would create a global profitable cartel to help our poor. Do you understand that, Akram? We estimated that our GDP growth could touch even thirteen percent with some of these advantages."

The PM sat down on the closest chair and took a sip of water.

"During all of this, the Chinese put in a clause in the trade agreement that we would disclose all our intelligence assets, so they could be given safe passage. You can't have secrets between partners, can you? they said to us. Our General sahib here did not like it one bit. He knew of course that we had a damn good operation going on in China under your command. CDC also raised a red flag suspecting the Chinese knew something.

"Around that time, another development took place. The local police in Dharamsala arrested a twenty-seven-year-old Chinese man with heroin. They sent a message through the local foreign office that he claimed he was the son of a high-ranking Chinese government employee. When we got to know he was Liu Rongji's son, we felt here was an excellent opportunity. Without informing the Chinese embassy, we contacted Liu and we started engaging with him. We knew that if word got out of his son's actions, his government would surely terminate his services and maybe even have his son assassinated here in India. Liu was most cooperative. About a month back, he gave an incredible piece of information that there was a leak out of RAW offices in India. He claimed that Mr Swamy and several team mates had been compromised and had started releasing information.

"Alarms went off, CDC knew Freddy well and confided in him. Freddy of course laughed it off. But CDC was concerned. Ministry of Defence SPOC for your project, Mr Khan, had updated CDC of your assets. We were worried that if indeed the information was correct, then who all were compromised? What of our assets in China and Taiwan? You may not be aware that there are three more countries where such a project is run. We were worried about compromising these assets. The task was now to surreptitiously get the A list of the agents and relocate them to a safe location without involving RAW. It was a very tough task. We could not inform you, lest you were already compromised, but the asset activation codes were in RAW. A plan was hatched to get someone from data management centre to infiltrate your unit and extract the list. As the assets would not cooperate with us and as they would assume we are the ones who were the enemy, we agreed to forcibly extract them. For their own safety, and of course, to make sure they don't fall into Chinese government's hands.

"At that stage, CDC had a brilliant idea to use Liu Rongji. We had already contacted him and were assuring him of complete support to help his son.

"Armed with a small cache of funds, the CDC worked with Liu's personal security apparatus outside of the state machinery and we extracted each of the eighteen assets. Now, Liu insists to getting custody of his son and only then facilitating the safe passage of our eighteen assets."

PM took a deep breath.

"So that, son, was my complete disclosure. The fact that you are here obviously means you are still a loyal patriot. It's your turn now. I want full disclosure. Please. No more games. I am old and getting tired."

Akram was still absorbing all that he had just heard. His mind was in a blur. Freddy had indeed mentioned this Swamy sir controversy which Freddy only had debunked. He could only now make sense of what was happening. He felt the sincere tone in the PM's long dialogue. He was sure the PM was not lying. It was very different to get inputs about people and then form your opinion once you met them.

"Are you telling me that the A list was stolen to protect the assets as you felt I could have been compromised?"

The CDC immediately responded to Akram. "You, and god knows who else, Mr Khan. Do you understand that kind of information flow your team has been providing this country? Perhaps we don't appreciate it enough. The Nathula Pass adventure by the Chinese? You recall how our forces were already at full readiness a week prior. Your source had given us such specifics that it was almost a shock for the Chinese. Of course, we had to the make the usual media noise about it so that they didn't get suspicious. So we were just not sure what was happening. For a week, we had planned a strike on RAW and remove twenty-four of the executive committee. I was just confident of Freddy. Frankly, Freddy was the the first person in the team to ridicule any attempt to classify Mr Swamy as a traitor. He said that he had worked with him for over twenty years and run operations with him. Confused by all of this, PM sir had prioritised the safe passage of our eighteen assets in China. We didn't trust anyone, Akram, not even you. Please recall we were all under panic for almost a week."

CDC picked up the bottle of water and after a few swigs continued. "The other thing, Akram, we were worried about was the geo-political humiliation of being discovered. Imagine eighteen Indian spies arrested in China, or worse, eighteen spies killed in action in China. The international politics arena would be set afire. We would have China block countries and raging at us in all forums. From the victim of terrorism, we would soon turn into perpetrators of espionage on a large trading partner."

Akram decided that he had nothing to lose by being truthful. His story was much longer. Almost half an hour later, he had finished his summary.

"And that, sir, is my disclosure."

The CDC and PM were in complete awe by what they had heard. A tunnel under the RB and the fact that Akram's great-grandfather had been a freedom fighter!

After a minute of silence, the PM got up and placed his hand on Akram's shoulder.

"Son, I salute your great-grandfather. What a momentous discovery you have made. How proud I feel of what your family has done for this nation."

He gestured to Akram, "Your boys can remove the masks. I am on your side."

Akram motioned to his team and soon an incredulous bunch of RAW agents stood sheepishly in front of the PM.

From balaclava-clad fierce terrorists, they looked like a bunch of college kids caught while trying to climb the college wall.

Akram responded to the PM, "Sir, we need to move fast for our assets."

"Yes, how do we convince Mr Liu to give up the locations?"

Akram reacted, "Sir, please allow me to speak with Liu. Norbu, get him in."

The PM nodded. He was struck with awe at the story he had just heard from a RAW officer whose great-grandfather had been a staunch freedom fighter. He couldn't wait to hear the details of how our freedom fighters managed to achieve such incredible feats. Getting the British to build the tunnel. A smile broke out on the PM's wrinkled brow and he almost broke out in laughter. Hey Prabhu! We are so lucky to be born in India. What an incredible breed of people. God bless us all, he thought to himself.

Norbu went outside, and in a minute, escorted Liu Rongji back.

"Mr Rongji, you heard our PM. From chaos will emerge a marvel. You have been of immense help. I am Akram Khan and those eighteen are under my watch. If anyone even gets injured Mr Rongji, I will personally execute your son on camera in front of you. We are peace-loving people, but we know how to make sacrifices. I suggest the following. I will stay in your custody with your personal security team at any location. My team will escort you and your son to Myanmar at a location I will give you. You will fly all my assets to the same location. Once the exchange has happened, we will all go home."

The CDC sprang up, "Myanmar? That's impossible Akram!"

"Relax sir, I know what I am doing. You were trained there, remember?"

CDC recalled a training programme at the RAW centre in Myanmar. Oh, that's smart. Liu will also be comfortable with Myanmar.

Liu thought about it and responded, "I agree with Mr Khan. This is a fair process. Let's do it, Mr Khan. PM sir... General sahib, *main aapse maafi mangta hu. Bacche hi sab kuch hai hamara, hai na?"*

The PM smiled, "Ji haan, Liu sahib. You are lucky that your son actually did not sell anything. He planned to procure but he was nabbed before he could do anything, so we could not have really run any case against him."

Mr Rongji smiled, "Aha, so you did outsmart me, Mr Prime Minister. I am glad Mr Akram was able to solve this problem. I thank you. Of course, you do know that if ever the Chinese government get to know that I helped these eighteen escape, I will be hanged."

"Don't worry, Liu sahib. Your secret is safe with us. Just make sure our children come back to us as well. Akram's team has been authorised to execute the plan. This has our government's blessings."

Akram nodded to Norbu who was commanded to accompany them with four of his team members.

"Norbu, you carry on. I don't think we have a snatch here tonight!"

"Aye, aye sir. Noted. No snatch but we are getting the team back, sir."

Both of them hugged and Akram slapped Norbu on his shoulders.

"Go ahead, Mr Liu. Norbu here is a fluent speaker of four Chinese dialects. His team will be the security detail with you. Your security detail will stay with me. Please do be aware that any attempt to play any kind of game will be met with severe action."

CDC had used his phone to alert the security outside. Norbu too had asked the full team to gather in the coffee service area. All the RB security staff were released.

The General looked at Norbu.

"So boys, please note that this was all planned as a mock drill. I have already updated the RB security. Please show the security chief the tunnel gate. For now, we will seal it."

"Indeed, but I want to launch this tunnel as a spectacular effort of Indian genius. Having the British build a tunnel that would have been used by our freedom fighters. Amazing. Akram ji, with your permission, I would want your Didima to be present and we will remember dearly our unrecognised hero of this fantastic architecture, Mr... Mr... sorry."

"Shri Prodipto Sengupta, sir," Akram shared his great-grandfather's name.

"I wonder, had the tunnel been used, perhaps our independence could have advanced to 1918. Why was it never used?"

"That sir," Akram responded"...is another story that Didima can tell you over some masala chai."

The PM laughed out loudly, "Yes, indeed. Akram, you truly represent the ethos of India. In your veins course the blood of so many cultures and yet together today, you Akram Khan were willing to teach a lesson to anyone who was not loyal to our desh, our Bharat.